D1624592

Death

and the

Butterfly

ALSO BY COLIN HESTER

Diamond Sutra
(reissued as *Diamonds and the Ten Thousand Things*)

Death
and the
Butterfly

A Novel

Colin Hester

COUNTERPOINT
Berkeley, California

"Death and the Butterfly" epigraph copyright © 2020 by Colin Hester and
David Allan Cates

English-to-German translations courtesy Dr. Johanna Timm

English-to-Spanish translations courtesy David Allan Cates and Ms. Roselia
Arellano-Sandoval

"Stand by Your Man." Words and music by Tammy Wynette and Billy Sherrill.
Copyright © 1967 (renewed) EMI Al Gallico Music Corp. Exclusive print
rights administered by Alfred Music. All rights reserved. Used by permission of
Alfred Music.

"My Heroes Have Always Been Cowboys." Words and music by Sharon
Vaughn. Copyright © 1976, 1980 Universal—Polygram International
Publishing, Inc. Copyright renewed. All rights reserved. Used by permission.
Reprinted by permission of Hal Leonard LLC.

Library of Congress Cataloging-in-Publication Data
Names: Hester, Colin, 1951– author.
Title: Death and the butterfly : a novel / Colin Hester.
Description: First hardcover edition. | Berkeley, California : Counterpoint,
    2020.
Identifiers: LCCN 2019026332 | ISBN 9781640093256 (hardcover) | ISBN
    9781640093263 (ebook)
Classification: LCC PR6058.E725 D43 2020 | DDC 823/.914—dc23
LC record available at https://lccn.loc.gov/2019026332

Jacket design by Sarah Brody
Book design by Wah-Ming Chang

COUNTERPOINT
2560 Ninth Street, Suite 318
Berkeley, CA 94710
www.counterpointpress.com

Printed in the United States of America

10 9 8 7 6 5 4 3 2 1

Above the battlefield,
Death and the butterfly
dance with the fallen.

—ANONYMOUS (translated from the Japanese)

Contents

I

SUNDERLAND

One

Finned—like iron sharks—the bombs slid out of the belly of the plane and into the night, coursing downward in scent of the city beneath.

They did not take long to find the ground. And to the two Luftwaffe fliers in the cockpit of the twin-engined Dornier 17, the bombs caused several small gray eruptions on the landscape beneath, at this altitude no more significant than the plops of frogs in a pond. Nor did the fliers hear any sound: not from the bombs they had unleashed nor even the endless hammering of the Daimler-Benz engines, for the two had long ago ceased hearing anything in the cockpit save each other's voices. They were clad in leather headgear and leather jackets, and now that the bombs had registered their seemingly inconsequential puffs, the pilot frowned and returned his attention to the task of flying. The other airman had unfolded navigational charts in a cascade across his lap, and with his gloved hands in the tight confines he began to somewhat awkwardly refold them.

After a moment the pilot turned to him. His face was solemn, and he said over the roar of the engines:

"Das ist London."[1]

"Nein, Herr Major," the navigator replied. He again unfolded the chart and lifted it slightly towards the pilot and pointed with a gloved finger to coordinates upon it, saying:

"Das sind die East End docks."[2] He then pointed to the instrument panel arrayed above their heads—to the gauge marked KOMPASS.

The pilot ignored the gauge. "Die East End docks von wegen!"[3] he said. He moved the rudder slightly to the left, and the plane dipped. Below, the gray eruptions caused by the bombs had crested and now began to settle. The plane leveled, and the pilot faced straight ahead. "Strikter Befehl vom Führer persönlich: eine Bombardierung von London ist verboten."[4]

"Es ist *nicht* London, Herr Major."[5]

"Lass uns das nur hoffen, Willy, sonst wird es uns nämlich sehr viel schlimmer ergehen als den armen Engländern!"[6]

Dipping a wing once more, the pilot managed a final look at the ground below. It had quiesced—as if in its stillness it had never been disturbed.

1. This is London.
2. No, Herr Major. This is the East End docks.
3. The East-End docks my arse.
4. The Fuhrer himself has strictly forbidden the bombing of London.
5. It is *not* London, Herr Major.
6. Let us both hope, Willy, otherwise our fate will be far worse than that of even the wretched English!

Two

"You mean, they bombed the City?" she heard her mother ask her father as the two of them came *clop-clop* down the staircase from upstairs.

"Not just in a bull's-eye but a calf's," her father said. "And now I've five bloody schools to send packing."

Her name was Susan, and she was in her slip in the kitchen rinsing her father's beloved spoon that she always fancied and snuck for her own tea. Silver-handled. The silver engraved: ROYAL AIR CORPS, '17–'18. She heard their shoe-heels drubbing the hallway floorboards.

"The Germans bombed *people?*"

They entered the kitchen. She looked up. Her mother, full-figured in her Sunday-best suede with her brown hair drawn back and pinned. Her father, in the gray weskit and pants of his pinstripe suit with starched collar and tie.

"Morning, love," her father said to her.

"Morning, Mac."

"Susan," her mother scolded her, "would you please stop calling him 'Mac.'"

"Phillip does," she said, referring to her older brother.

"Phillip's in the RAF," her mother said. "And will you for God's sake get some clothes on!"

"What's wrong with this slip?" she said.

"You're thirteen," her mother said. "That's what's wrong with it."

"Oh, Cless," her father countered, "thirteen by only a day or two." He crossed the few steps to her. "She's still a child." He kissed her on the cheek. "How's me spoon?" he asked her.

"I'm wearing it away," she said.

"Like the Cliffs of Dover," her father said.

"Mac, you—you said *five* schools?" her mother asked her father.

Just above the sink was a window that gave out to the house of their neighbors—the Tranters—and in that windowglass Susan caught the palest of her own reflections: large dark eyes—almost chocolate—a classic English nose, and ample lips so thick and lush they might have bestowed a kiss on Providence itself. On her head, a beautiful entanglement of blackening hair. Shoulder-length. Beside her reflection in the windowglass, a white linen towel hung from a wall hook and Susan whipped the towel off the hook and gave the spoon a quick once-over.

"Five schools?" her mother repeated. "But that's, what, fifteen hundred children?"

"Fifty buses," her father corrected. She handed her father

his spoon. "Ta," he whispered and gave her another quick peck on the cheek. "How's the tea coming along?" he asked her.

"Tar sands," she said.

"Grand," he said. He paused, mock frowning. "At least I think so," he said. He turned to her mother. "Anyroad, let's have a cup, Cless," he said. "And any biscuits?"

Susan had minutes before cobbled out the teacups and the saucers on the kitchen table, all arrayed around the cozied teapot. Now, her mother unhooded the cozy and one-handed hoisted the pot and tipped it and spooled the dark amber into her father's cup and then she set the cozy back atop the teapot and did so with the reverence of one performing the investiture of a raj. Done, her mother stepped to the pantry and clicked on the light.

"And any cheese, Cless?" her father said.

"So they bombed people?" her mother said.

"I already told you. And you can rest assured the Old Lion will give them back a taste of their own. Tonight, if I'm not surprised."

"Maybe it'll be Phillip," Susan suggested.

"Phillip doesn't fly bombers," her father said.

"Phillip doesn't fly anything yet," her mother said.

"A week or two away from his wings," her father said. He sipped his tea. "So, any cheese, Cless?"

"There's Stilton."

"Oh, Christ, no," her father said. "It'll give me gas."

"You've always got gas," her mother said. She ducked out of the pantry and clicked off the light and closed the pantry door. She handed the cake-tin of biscuits to her husband.

"Angels," Susan said, not quite to herself.

"Angels don't get gas," her mother said.

"They would if they ate Stilton," her father said.

"Mac," her mother scolded. "Don't be impious. It's Sunday."

With his two thumbs her father popped the lid of the biscuit tin and peered inside—seriously so, as if the individual biscuits therein might be of widely varying quality.

"It may indeed be bloody Sunday," her father said, "but it's not *my* bloody day of rest, is it?" He snapped shut the biscuit tin without making any particular decision. Thoughtful for a moment. Her father looked at her. "Angels?" he repeated to her. "Don't you get religious on me too. One's enough."

"No. What you said about Phillip getting his wings. The way angels supposedly earn theirs."

"Indeed," he said, "indeed," a wave of worry now quickening his face. He frowned at some distant space.

"What, Dad?"

"Nothing. Nothing."

"Susan," her mother said. "Go upstairs, please."

"Let—let her stay, Cless."

"Susan!"

"For God's sake—"

"Susan!"

"Cless, let her stay. It's—it's about Phillip and his wings."

"What—what about them? About Phillip, I mean."

"If he gets them—*when* he gets them . . ."

"Yes?"

"Well, he—he earns leave."

Her mother trembled for a moment then made a fist and stood it on the hip of her skirt. "Leave?" she said. "Leave? And you kept this from me?"

"*He* kept it from you."

"But he'd never."

"Yes, Cless. He did. In case there's a snag and, well, you're disappointed."

"But when?" Susan asked.

"Susan!" her mother said. "Know your place."

"He gets leave somewhere over the next fortnight," her father told her mother, "if—if he gets his—" her father glanced at her then returned his attention to her mother, "—the chance."

"Leave," her mother repeated softly. She shook her head in disbelief. She kept a small handkerchief stowed under the sleeve of her Sunday jacket and she plicked it out and dabbed the corner of each of her eyes. "Let's pray he gets the chance," she said.

"Finally," her father said, "one prayer I'm all in favor for."

Three

Through this second-story window, you could see the tall iron palings of the palace's fence and then the twin columns of the North-End gate. Beyond the gate a double-decker bus, freighted and tippy with waving youngsters and belongings, tacked like a high red dory around the stone of the Victoria Memorial and headed northeast, leaving the Mall. A man stood at the window watching the bus. He was stocky, his facial features at once blunt and fierce, and watching the bus's departure he frowned, then after a moment reconsidered and smiled. Behind him a door opened and he turned to find a servant—his head bowed—holding it open as a slim man with weary eyes entered. The slim man was attired in the olive-cloth uniform of a British Army officer and he began to speak—or rather attempted to do so, for the words seemed elusive to him like a rainbow in an aviary.

"Puh—*Prime* Minister," the uniformed man finally managed.

"Your Majesty," the man at the window—Winston Churchill of course—said and he bowed and the servant stepped back and out into the hallway and closed the door.

The room the two men inhabited was small, decorated white with Victorian chairs, a high but shallow Rumford fireplace and a large portrait in oil of Admiral Nelson above the mantel. From the ceiling hung a modest chandelier that glittered even in the late-afternoon light and by the fireplace was a tall mahogany cart on wheels. On the cart awaited cut-crystal glasses and varicolored bottles and a trio of swan-necked crystal decanters, and the man in the uniform—George, king of England, emperor of India—gestured expansively towards the tray and said, "Cognac?"

"If Your Majesty is having one."

"I am."

The king crossed the cashmere of the carpet as soundlessly as a shadow and slid forth two large snifters. He selected a black long-necked bottle—its base stout as a Dickensian squire—and he poured first one then another drachm then repeated it so they had doubles. He set the bottle back in its slot and picked up the snifters, holding them where the scoop of their large bowls met their stems and with one in each palm he walked to the man by the window and said with effort yet with slow and careful clarity, "If we had a fire, my dear Winston, we might warm them."

The king handed Churchill his brandy. They both swirled their drinks, the liquid snatching in dark orange flames at the flawless crystal glass.

"There is warmth enough in this great palace, Your Majesty," Churchill told the king, "to anneal a thousand such glasses."

Standing there by the window, they lifted their glasses and drank.

"I've been watching the buses of children drive by," the king said.

"And?"

"And, they wave."

"And does Your Majesty wave back?"

"Yes. Though doing so troubles me."

"Why is that, Majesty?"

"Hmmm? Oh." The king placed his brandy snifter on the windowsill and dug into his trouser pockets for his silver cigarette case. Withdrawing it, he used his thumb to press its release and it unfolded in his palm. The cigarettes were Turkish plain ends—that is, unfiltered—and were initialed G. R. He selected one and with the lighter built into the spine of the case lit it. He took a deep pull from his cigarette allowing, as he took it from between his lips, the release of a small fist of smoke that he immediately re-inhaled. Once held deeply in his lungs, he blew out the smoke slowly in a long dancing fringe that in the window's embrasure lingered, a shimmering isthmus.

Churchill remained quiet.

The king now addressed Churchill's earlier question:

"Why does the children's waving, and my own, bother me, you asked?"

"Yes, Majesty."

The king looked away from the window and looked tiredly at Churchill. "Because I—I can't decide if they're waving hello or—" (and here he groped for the enunciation) "—or guh—*good*bye."

"I'd prefer to think they are waving both their loyalty and their love, Your Majesty."

The king considered this, then said:

"I need an ashtray." He walked to the fireplace and fetched one and returned, taking another deep drag on his cigarette. He set the ashtray onto the windowsill beside his snifter of cognac. He exhaled in precisely the same way he had done moments before, and he scooped up his snifter and drank. Churchill did likewise.

The king said:

"The bombing of London last night."

"Yes?"

"You think it unintended?"

"I think it an error," Churchill said. "Navigational perhaps—let the historians wrangle and gather clues—but a grave error, an error that will cost the Germans dearly."

"The bombing of Berlin?"

"The loss of the war, Your Majesty."

The king very slowly placed his snifter back on the windowsill. He straightened and looked directly at Churchill and asked, "How?"

"I intend," Churchill told him, "to retaliate not just once, tit for tat as they say, but repeatedly."

"Repeatedly?"

"Every night, Your Majesty, and of Berlin."

"But—but why?"

"Your Majesty, our Number Eleven Fighter Group has received extensive damage at five of their forward airfields, not to mention the six sector stations. On the Kentish coast, Majesty, Lympne and Manston—well, for days, unfit for our fighters to operate from. As for our field south of London—"

"Biggin Hill?"

"Yes, Majesty."

"What of it?"

"For the past week, it's been so damaged that only one fighter squadron could operate from it." Churchill paused, then continued. "Your Majesty, we have lost—*lost* the Battle of Britain."

"Lost?"

"Yes. But we shall win—*win* the War of London."

"How?"

"By our incessant retaliation of last night's mistake. And, in doing so, by goading Hitler and his strutting Air Marshal Goering into changing their plan of attack from England's military targets—our air defense targets, our precious and heavily damaged air fields—change their attacks from those targets to—to England herself."

The king thought for a second. The cigarette in his hand emitted a soft undulating crimp of smoke and turning to the window he crushed it in the ashtray. He took a moment then faced Churchill.

"You mean London?" he said with no unmarked gravity. "The City itself?"

Churchill nodded.

"The people themselves?"

Churchill remained silent, motionless.

"Good God," the king said.

Four

"Irony," Miss Reddish repeated. "Susan?"

"Sorry—oh, sorry, Miss." She was standing in the class-room aisle by her desk—her Reader lesson book was open on it—and she glanced quickly down at it then back at Miss Reddish, who stood at the side of the class, the windows behind her. In the far distance beyond the windows was the dying hum of an airplane. "It was the sound of the plane, Miss Reddish," she told her. "Its engines."

"I can assure you, Miss McEwan, that after our bombing of Berlin this fortnight past, it is not an unfriendly plane."

"Of course, Miss."

"So. Continue."

"With irony?"

"If you can do so without being overly ironic," Miss Reddish said.

Early autumn. The classroom windows were open and they rendered forth the scent and slow decay of all the trees just beyond them. It had been raining but now the rain had ceased and as the grind of the plane's engines withered she could hear the *drip-drip* of the drops as they relinquished their grip on the leaves. Miss Reddish wore a midlength black scholar's gown and she took off her glasses and held them in both her hands and she walked from the window and stood in front of the clean, almost-polished chalkboard.

"Irony," she said.

Susan cleared her throat. "Do you mean poetic irony, Miss, or the irony of fate?"

Miss Reddish raised an eyebrow and for an instant considered Susan from beneath it. "You *have* read your Fowler," she said, "haven't you?"

"Yes, Miss."

"Quite. It seems you're well on your way to being our beloved isle's next great poet."

"Miss?"

"The irony of fate, Susan. The irony of fate."

Susan collected her thoughts. The class was extraordinarily quiet—these thirty or so thirteen-year-old uniformed boys and girls. They seemed expectant as if seeking some revelation from Susan, hopefully spiced with mild scandal. She did not disappoint:

"Well, my brother, Phillip—my older brother—he's, well, he hates water."

"A hydrophobe."

"Sorry, Miss, but doesn't that mean he's *scared* of water?"

"There's no shame in fearing something, Susan."

"Of course not, Miss."

"When you fear something, you cede it its due respect."

"Yes, Miss. Well, he hates water, Phillip does, and so when the war broke out he refused to join the navy and instead signed on with the RAF."

"Does he fly Spitfires?" the boy sitting beside her blurted out.

"Stuart!" Miss Reddish snapped.

"Sorry," the boy muttered.

"Proceed, Susan."

"So, he hates water, shuns the Royal Navy, and signs on with the RAF—and here's the irony—they're supposed to assign him to fly Sunderlands."

"Flying boats," Miss Reddish said.

"Yes, Miss."

Miss Reddish considered this. She wore very high heels and their *noohk-noohk* was the only sound as she walked from in front of the blackboard towards the open windows. There, she stopped and turned to the class. "So he hasn't won his wings yet," she said.

"Oh, yes. A few days since. And he's earned leave."

"You'll get to see our heroic flier?"

"He arrives today, Miss."

"Ahh."

"And tomorrow he'll take me to the bathing pool. For my birthday."

"And how do you know he will?"

"He does every year, Miss."

"Takes you swimming? This heroic and hydrophobic flier

19

of ours?" Miss Reddish said. "He *also* has a grand sense of the ironic, doesn't he, class?"

"Yes, Miss," they all but Susan choired back.

"Then I should think he deserves a tribute." She turned and gazed out the window, pensive. Through the distant cloud cover, like a once-withdrawing wave returning to the shore, the plane's engine began to become audible again. A breeze shivered the leaves of the trees and more captured raindrops were released to fall and splatter on the pavement. Miss Reddish faced the class again.

"Yes, a tribute. Assuring each and every one of you completes his or her sums correctly, an early dismissal."

The boys and girls all stared at their neighbors, disbelief widening all their eyes.

"Indeed, a tribute," Miss Reddish announced. "Well, class, shut your Reader lesson books and get out your sums books. Apparently, one or two of you have a war to salvage and a birthday to celebrate."

Five

It *had* to be Phillip's, the motorbike—an Ariel—that was parked by the curb as she came up the walk from school. It was bullet-colored, that dull flat deathly gray, and it had a stubby sidecar and the other traffic on this side of the street that passed by—a black taxi, a tiny Morris Minor, a tilting bus—did so very closely and she was faster and faster walking up the front path now, the grass a deep green on either side. In those days the doors of English houses had neither door handles nor latches—only key-entry dead bolts—so she slipped the straps of her school satchel off her shoulders, and resting the satchel on the doorstep she unbuckled its front mini-pouch and wiggled out her door key, and as quietly as she could she inserted her key and unlocked and opened the door. As she did, within the door's slender cut-glass panes she could see the many crystalline images of the front hall that she stepped inside of and into. She was almost out of breath but she could hear voices from the kitchen, some she didn't recognize:

"Thanks, Mrs. McEwan, but I'm meeting a girl, I'm afraid."

"There, Phillip, you *see?*"

"Mother!"

"Your son's too picky, Mrs. McEwan, that's the problem."

"Oh, bugger off, Roger."

Soundlessly she closed the door behind her back. She set her satchel on the floor by the brolly basket, hung her snouted gas mask on the coat tree, and continued to listen while slowly and quietly approaching the kitchen.

"No matter how good-looking they are, Mrs. McEwan," yet another male voice told her mother, "he says they're all U-S."

"American?"

"RAF-speak, Mum," Phillip explained. "As in unsuitable. Roger and Nial here may be *on* leave, but they never really leave."

"Hello, then!" Roger announced, seeing Susan standing in the kitchen doorway.

She looked at them. Her mum over by the sink in a puffy-sleeved blouse and pleated skirt—both cream-colored—with a glass of sherry, holding its stem like a recently cut flower. And Phillip and Roger and Nial down by the window, each of them holding sherry glasses as well and leaning a free hand on the iron shoulder of the laundry mangle. Behind them through the window, the garden—as English gardens strangely are— was, in the overcast, a deeper green than even when the sun shone.

As for Phillip and Roger and Nial, they were in their pastel-gray RAF uniforms, each with the winged insignia on his left lapel like a white feather or flame.

"You didn't tell me you'd an older sister, Phillip," Roger said. He was tall and lank with a lion of blond hair and otherwise craggishly handsome and he straightened like a coil of rope brought to life. Sipping slowly from his sherry glass, he appraised her standing there in the doorway, never allowing his eyes—which were a soft Cadbury brown—to leave her body or her own eyes.

She looked down at the floor.

"Why, love," her mother said, "you're home early."

"I—I told class about Phillip," she said to her mother before finally looking at her brother.

Ah, her brother. He had thick wavy hair that he combed straight back, and his eyes, because of his dark brows, seemed almost locked if not in a frown then in puzzlement. The rest of his face was good-looking enough, so her girlfriends said, to overcome this shadow upon his features and he said to her, softly:

"Susan!" and blindly passed his sherry glass to Nial who took it, and he crossed the kitchen and took her hands and kissed her one cheek then the other.

She stood on her tiptoes while he did, though she'd no need.

"You're still here," he said.

"Not evacuated," she said, "*yet*." She nicked a quick glance at Phillip's other mate: not quite as tall as Roger but less angular and with the rain-dark hair and flutter-giver smile of a potentially truant choirboy.

"If your dad'd let me," her mother told Phillip, "I'd have her up in Godmanchester in a minute."

"What?" Phillip said. "Uncle Cec's?"

"His brother-in-law, Ben's."

"The smithy?"

Susan still held Phillip's hands, and she said his name and asked:

"Can—can we go swimming?" She came down onto her heels and looked away, and her eyes met Roger's once again.

"Swimming?" her brother repeated.

"Yes," she said. "Tomorrow?"

He touched her chin, looking at her gently. "I can't say," he said.

"Why—why ever not?"

He thought for a moment. "Well, Roger and Nial, they cadged the Ariel."

"The motorbike?"

"We've it *un*officially."

"Our own two-man den of thieves," Nial said.

"True enough," Roger said. "Though we two thieves have no need for it."

She glanced across at him. Her mother said:

"But Captain Grey, I thought you were meeting a girl."

"I am," Roger said. "But she has a car."

"My word," her mother said. "That's rather posh."

"Actually, Mrs. McEwan," Nial said, "she has several."

"There, you see?" Roger said. "If Saint Nial himself said it, it must be true. So take it," Roger insisted, and as he did, behind him in the garden the sun came out briefly; then the shade returned. "Hold on," he said, coming across the kitchen. As Phillip let go of Susan, Roger said: "I—"

Roger stopped, looking at her.

"What?" she asked.

Roger didn't say anything.

"What is it, Captain Grey?" her mother said.

"Hmm?"

"Captain?"

"*Don't*, Roger," Nial cautioned, "all right?"

"Oh, shush, little brother. Well?"

Roger hadn't taken his eyes from hers. They could all hear the front door click open.

"S'that Dad?" Phillip asked, turning to face the hallway.

"You're cross-eyed," Roger told her.

"What?" Phillip said.

"Mmn," Roger nodded.

The front door opened. "Phillip?" her father called.

"*Cross*-eyed?" Phillip repeated.

She heard the anger in Phillip's voice. She immediately lowered her eyes and heard her father step inside and close the front door and call again, "Phillip? Phillip?"

"He's in here, Mac," her mother said. "Captain Grey's only saying what he thinks he sees, Phillip."

"*Cross-eyed?*" Phillip said once more.

"Yes," Roger said, "but barely. I'd never've caught it but when she looked across at me, the sudden sunlight in the window—"

"Roger," Nial said in a lowered voice but equally as emphatic, "this is his sister."

"My thirteen-year-old sister," Phillip added and said to Roger, "not one of your—"

"Phillip!" her father called, coming down the hall. "Son!"

He wore his brown pinstripe, weskited and with a lighter brown tie under his stark white shirt.

"Hello, Father," Phillip said.

Her father stood in the kitchen doorway, blinking, his eyes moist. "What's this 'Father' business?" he asked his son.

"Sorry, *Dad.*"

"It's Mac to you now, son—Mac."

"All right. Fine. Mac, then."

Her father held out his hand, and her brother took it and was at once hauled in to a half embrace, half pat on the back. Her father stepped back. For some moments he looked at his son. He shook his head ever everso slowly. Shut his eyes and opened them again that he might see his son, taste with his eyes the very life of this man, this flier, his pride. Which he did. Sighing, he looked at Roger, at Nial, then back at Phillip.

"This is Captain Grey," her mother announced—Roger bowed his head—"and Flight Lieutenant McKellan,"—who did likewise.

Her father extended his hand and first Nial took it and shook it and then Roger.

"What," Roger said with a grin, "no hugs for us?"

Her father frowned in puzzlement.

"It's just him, Da—*Mac*," Phillip said.

"Take no notice, Mr. McEwan," Nial said.

Her father and Roger were still shaking hands and then her father yanked Roger towards him, as if to indeed give him a hug and Roger in trying to avoid it stumbled on his own feet like a calf and Nial and her brother and father laughed, though warmly. Susan too was smiling, as was her mother.

"We're having sherries," her mother said.

"Damn," her father said, glancing at his watch. "Why can't it be five?"

"Oh, go on," her mother said, "it won't hurt you."

"Rules are rules," he said. He looked at Susan. "Hello, love," he said. "You must be feeling dreadfully ignored."

"Actually, no," she answered, blinking several times.

"Rules are made to be broken, Mr. McEwan," Roger said.

"*Hearts* are made to be broken, Captain Grey," her father said.

"Please, it's Roger."

"Roger, then. Rules aren't even meant to be bent."

"And I'd agree, Mr. McEwan," Nial said.

"Well, I'm siding with Roger," her mother said. "This isn't London Transport. Once isn't going to hurt, for *Lord's* sake."

"I doubt He's having one," her father said.

"How d'you know? Perhaps He might. And Susan will have one too. Love? Yes?"

She looked at her mother then her father.

"Oh, all right," her father said, "corrupt your child as well then. And your Lord God in His ludicrous Heaven." He crossed the kitchen and stood beside her mother and then kissed her quickly on the cheek. "What's next, I don't know."

"A glass of the driest," her mother answered. With her hand she smoothed her skirt across her thighs and crossed the kitchen to the table. The sherry bottle was there on it, standing sleek and tall and darkly opaque and there were three extra long-stemmed glasses and her mother lifted the bottle and uncorked it and began filling one of the glasses with the honey-colored wine. "Then Captain Grey is meeting a girl," she said. "One with a car."

Her father nodded in approval and sipped his sherry and glanced at Nial. "And surely you too, Flight Lieutenant?"

"Merely the third wheel, I'm afraid," Nial said.

"This—this girl," Susan interrupted, asking Roger. "Is *she* cross-eyed?"

Roger grinned. "All my girls are," he said.

Six

"Then why'd he say so?" she asked, gripping the edge of the swimming pool and pushing herself up and out of the water. As she did, the pool water slipped down her body like a negligée.

Sideways she sat on the pool's edge, her slender legs, from mid-calves downward, immersed. The swimming baths—the pool—were crowded as a holiday camp and as noisy. Here in the deep end there were twin five-meter diving platforms and a low springboard which tongued out above the water. Above them, the high windows all around the walls steamed. Close by on the deck Phillip lay on his side, on a towel, his chest and legs quite white, his maroon bathing trunks quite dry.

"Because that's his line," he told her.

"His line?" she asked, imprisoning a stray strand of her hair back under her bathing cap.

"Yes. How he picks up girls," Phillip said.

"How would lying to them that they're cross-eyed let him—"

Came then a shriek! as someone in the pool raised a great showering splash that in an arc raked and hailed down on the two of them and she ducked and winced and instantly Phillip recoiled and rolled away from its icy sparks and scrambled to his feet.

She looked around at the perpetrator. "Stuart!" she exclaimed.

It was the boy from her class. "Sorry, Susan," he said, "sorry! It was an accident, honest." He was treading water and doing so inefficiently, his neck arched back so that he barely kept it above water. He sniffed.

"Stuart," she said, "you are so—so *un*ironic."

"I know," he said. "Is that your boyfriend, then?" he asked, his arms and legs pedaling away in the water.

"My brother," she answered.

Phillip approached the pool's edge, bending swift and lean to scoop up his towel.

"The one who's scared of water?" Stuart asked.

"Stuart!" Susan shouted.

"It's all right, love," Phillip said.

"Well, you did tell us in class," Stuart blundered on.

"One more," Susan warned him, "and I'm in the water and wringing your miserable neck."

Stuart poked his tongue out at her.

"Now you've copped it," she said.

"Don't, love," Phillip said. He yoked his towel around his neck and tugged her arm. "Here," he said, "I've something to show you."

She peeled her bathing cap from her head and tossed out

her hair. "Oh, all right," she said, and she and Phillip wove hopscotching through the bodies lying on towels that littered the pool's deck.

"DO THEY ALL FANCY YOU?" Phillip asked her outside by the motorcycle. Though there were clouds, they were high and intermittent, and the sun shone warmly on them. He handed her the leather helmet and goggles she was to wear and he unfastened and peeled back the black canvas tonneau of the sidecar. Streaming past in the road was a steady river of traffic and once they'd both threaded their heads into the helmets and donned the channel-swimmer-like goggles, Phillip mounted the Ariel, and she slid snuggly into the sidecar and did so as effortlessly as if descending a playground slide.

"Where are we going?" she asked.

"To see my battlefield," he answered.

The Ariel started on first kick, loud and rabbling, and Phillip pushed it off by its handgrips and danced the big machine into the traffic. Susan adjusted her goggles on the bridge of her nose then said above the engine's roar:

"And you can tell Roger that even my goggles are cross-eyed."

FROM NORTH CHEAM THEY RAN the Ariel due east across the north lip of the City, and once beyond central London they curved south, catching up with the Thames near the East End docks. Then, running parallel to the great river's voltas, they headed east through Rainham and Erith and Grays. The Thames here was as wide as a sea—indeed, it had miles earlier become tidal—and past the town of Grays, Phillip shouted, "Hungry?" and she answered, "Yes, famished," and he carried on through Coryton and South Benfleet and she shouted at him, "Phillip, I thought we were stopping!" and he shouted back, "We are! We are!" but he didn't stop, didn't stop until, with the engine beneath them pawing at the air, he double-clutched and machine-gun downshifted and into the lovely village of Canvey they did sweep.

It was not quite three o'clock and though the shops were closed he found a caffey—as the English pronounced and spelled "café" in doughboy French—and pulled up in front.

The street was quiet. There were shops on one side, and on the other was the sea wall and then the beveled slope of the white sand that rippled down to the edge of the river. Disentangling themselves from the Ariel's viscera they stood on the sidewalk and peeled back their headgear and with deep breaths they smelled the warm yet somehow always cold air of the sea—that lonely almost leathery fragrance—and Phillip pulled open the caffey door. As he did so a small bell tingled above them and they entered.

There were three wooden tables without tablecloths, the wooden chairs around each of the tables tipped forward so that the chairs leaned on their front legs against the tables' edges. A Camp's Coffee advert hung on one sidewall and beside it was the menu chalkboard. On the caffey's other side was a serving counter and behind it, his back to them, a man in an apron was employing a washcloth to brush the crumbs from the preparation countertop into his cupped other hand.

"We're closed," the man said without turning.

"Oh," Phillip said to the man, "sorry," then to Susan, "Sorry, love." Phillip pulled open the door—the bell tingling again—and they reentered the sunshine and sea air.

"Well?" Phillip asked. He pushed the fingernails of both hands through his thick black hair and frowned, his dark brows almost touching above his handsome nose. Behind them the door shut; then they heard the bell ring, and puzzled at this reversal of order the two of them turned.

The shopkeep's apron was white and stained around the midsection. He had thin gray hair combed across the top of his head, and still holding the washcloth he gestured at Phillip and said, "Sorry. Didn't see you were in the service."

"That's all right," Phillip said, "it's just a uniform. Doesn't give us carte blanche to be a bother."

"Oh, you're not, young man, you're not. Please," he said, "come in, come in."

Susan told the man:

"We were just looking for a cup of tea and a sandwich. I'm sure we can wait till we get back."

The caffey owner looked at her for a long moment then at Phillip. "You've a right catch there, young officer."

"She's—"

The man held up a hand of discretion. "Tell you what, it's lovely and all, the day is. I'll fetch out a pair of chairs and set them on the sidewalk, Parisian-like, and I'll make you both a quick cup of and see if there's a cucumber sandwich or two."

"Really?" Phillip asked.

The man nodded, and in an instant he was back at the door with the two chairs. She and Phillip were smiling and Phillip held open the door as the man waggled the chairs past and stood them up so they faced the street. "You'll have to balance your cup and saucers on your legs, mind you," he said, "so careful you don't scald yourselves."

"Yes," they said, "thanks."

"My pleasure," he said. "Lucky there's no licensing laws for caffeys. Marmite?" he asked them.

They looked at each other.

"On your sandwiches," the man explained.

"Yes," Phillip said eagerly, "if you've some."

"I've still the jar I had before the war," the man told them.

And on the sidewalk by the quiet street in this ever so quiet Saturday village they sat side by side on the wooden caffey chairs, sat in the sun, watching the Thames shoulder its way into the channel while the man inside prepared their tea and sandwiches.

"What did you mean," she asked her brother, "by his *line*?"

"Whose?"

"Roger's!"

"Oh, that."

"Yes, that."

He looked at her. "Well, it's his method."

"Thought it was his line?"

"His *way*. His theory: belittle them in public, girls that is, then be nice to them in private."

She didn't say anything. And because the day was so clear

34

they could see across the undulating swell of the channel to France's coast, a thin raft of a horizon but visible.

"And does it work?" she asked her brother. "His method."

"He thinks so."

They were quiet for a moment.

"And the other?"

"Nial?"

"Does he use the same *method*?"

"Roger says Nial doesn't need to."

"Because he's so pretty?"

"Likely, though you'd never get Roger to admit to *that* part of it."

They were quiet. After a bit, Susan nodded towards the channel. "And this is *your* battlefield?" she asked him.

"Yes," he said.

A breeze picked up and it blew her hair slightly across her face and she cleared it away with a hand.

"Phillip," she said.

"Yes?"

"I'm sorry I told class about your . . . you know—"

"Water thing?"

"Yes."

He placed his hand on hers and kissed her quickly on the cheek. "That's all right," he said, "really. It's like telling them my—my shoe size. It doesn't matter."

"Really?"

He nodded. "That's why I love the Sunderlands. You get shot out of the sky, you've still got a boat between you and the water."

The caffey door opened with a tingling and the owner came out carrying a low wooden stool. On its flat top was a color print of Winnie-the-Pooh and Christopher Robin (C.R. in his Wellingtons), the print faded yet still recognizable, and the owner set it at their feet. "It was our Albert's," he said. "For your pot 'n cups. I couldn't stand the thought of one of our young fliers being scalded by me tea. Perhaps put out of action."

"I haven't seen any action, yet," Phillip said, "but the stool is marvelous."

"'Scuse my effrontery, Miss," the owner said, "but our Albert used it in the loo."

"Oh," Susan said, glancing at Phillip.

"As a step-up. When he was a little 'un."

"Yes," she said.

The owner straightened and turned to take in the day and the sea. He took a moment, looking. "There's clouds," he said, "coming from Calais. Dark ones, too."

"They won't reach us here, luckily," Phillip said. "The wind's from the west. It'll blow them back into Germany where they belong."

"Let's pray," the owner said, going back inside.

Phillip studied the clouds above the far coast of France, frowning.

"What is it?" she asked.

A bell tingled and they looked round, but the shop door hadn't opened; rather, in the street a young boy her age coasted by on his bicycle. The boy waved at her and rang his bell again.

Then again. Then it was quiet and they could almost hear the smell of the sea with its waves whispering across the sand of the shore. And too they could hear a soft and gentle hum, like bees at their gathering labor of buttercups.

"Phillip?" she said again but he didn't respond. He still watched the horizon, the clouds. Another bell tingled and this time the caffey door *did* open and they looked around and the owner emerged carrying a black lacquered tray. He stood before them and stooped slightly. "Here," he said. "Will you do the honors, young miss?"

"Yes," she said, "yes," and from the tray she hoisted first the cozied teapot and placed it on the Pooh stool then the two cups tilted one inside the other and both on the doubled-up saucers. She separated and arranged the cups and saucers then found room for the cucumber sandwiches. The crusts had been trimmed off.

"Ta," the owner said. He straightened and looked out across the water. The hum was louder now. "Dark as Marmite is that rain cloud," he said.

"It's not a rain cloud," Phillip said, his voice containing equal measures of matter-of-fact and sheer disbelief.

"No?" the owner asked. He stared at the cloud, then said, "No, no it's *not*."

It had taken minutes to become visible, then minutes to cast its noise of passage—its horrendous hum—but it surely seemed to the three of them there on the sidewalk with their pot of tea and Marmite sandwiches to take no longer than a heartbeat to swoop across the channel like an enormous lid of darkness, a wide and droning iron roof of war.

"Good Christ!" said Phillip.

Neither Phillip nor she nor the owner moved. The word "awe" has as its root the Icelandic word "agi," meaning the terror one experiences when one looks directly into the face of God. And it was indeed that awe, that terror that was on their faces as getting louder and louder the Heinkels and Dorniers and Messerschmitts and Fokkers roared towards and above them, the thousand-plane flotilla—a thousand planes!—forming in the sky a deafening and dark horde, a dark and relentless canopy of precision and death.

Their force was such that their passing overhead blew Phillip's RAF cap off and he snatched at it and Susan put her young hand atop her head as her own hair swirled in a tangle of silken wire and eyes raised she watched as if transfigured, her mouth open.

"They're following the Thames!" the owner shouted.

"To London!" Phillip cried. "They're following it straight to bloody London!"

THE SOUND OF THE BOMBS dropping (she and Phillip could not but hear that sound even above the Ariel's engine as they ran it west in their maniacal race back to the City), that sound was dull and muted and terrifying, like the thump of bodies being thrown endlessly one after another onto a charnel cart. Ahead of them on the horizon the sky filled with smoke, black pillars of it twisting up into the sky in desperation and there were sudden flames cast up in splashes of lurid red gore that settled like mirages and there was that forever dull and lifeless pounding, that pounding.

And the soft punching-bag sound of the City's few anti-aircraft guns and the Ariel's engine switching as Phillip geared up and down and sped back up and did so over and over again, but loudest of all, their thoughts, their thoughts.

Seven

The candle blew out and the tiny underground bomb shelter was dark, cold. They could hear the bombs whistling one after another as they fell to earth, howling like marauding Huns at the gates. Mrs. Tranter struck a match, and her face illuminated, blue and undulate as if inhabiting a gas flame. She rose as best she could, bent double, the roof of corrugated iron looming mere inches above her doubled-over spine. She two-stepped the dying match to the candle and managed to light it again and the shelter filled with wickering light.

She wagged out the match. The bombs that had whistled fell *poom! poom! poom!* and Susan's mother, sitting on the liner of the floor with legs splayed, propped her back against the post of twin bunks stacked low and tight as dresser drawers. She swung her purse onto her lap and from within salvaged a near-gone packet of Woodbines and snapped the purse shut and took out a cigarette and said:

"They're getting closer."

"D'you need the candle?"

"Ta. Thanks," her mother said.

She took the candle in its Arabian brass holder and lit her cigarette and passed the candle back to Mrs. Tranter.

Mrs. Tranter set the candle on top of the small army trunk that sat in the middle of the floor. "Where's Mac, then?" she asked.

"He'll be here soon," her mother said.

"Mum?" Susan asked.

"What, love?"

"Can we read Phillip's letter again?"

"No, love. We shouldn't have read it that once. Wait for your father."

She was silent.

"How *is* Phillip?" Mrs. Tranter asked. "If you don't mind my asking."

"Flying. And he's found a girlfriend," her mother told Mrs. Tranter.

"Mum?"

"Yes, love?"

"Are there any cakes left, then?"

"Yes."

Her mother took a deep drag of her cigarette, then let the smoke out slowly.

"May I have one? Please?"

"If you have a sandwich first," her mother said.

Again they could hear the staggered whistle-whistle-whistling as another cluster of bombs dropped from the sky, then the *poom! poom! poom!*

"What's left?" Susan asked.

There was a cake tin on the floor liner just by her mother, and her mother, her cigarette's smoke a dizzying contrail, took the tin and placed it in her lap and clawed open the lid. She poked inside. "Paste," she said.

"What kind?"

Her mother looked. "Sardine and tomato," she said.

Susan said nothing.

"Well?" her mother said.

"Is that all?"

"Yes, love, that's all. What's wrong with sardine and tomato?"

"It's just . . . well, it gives you terrible breath."

Her mother didn't say anything.

"We've corned beef?" Mrs. Tranter offered.

"Corned beef?" her mother said.

"Jimmy. He sends tins of it from Canada."

Her mother crushed her cigarette in the nearby glass ashtray. "Corned beef," her mother repeated.

"Yes."

"How—how's Etta?" her mother asked.

"Getting shuffled about. Now they've got her billeted with a family of Catholics." Mrs. Tranter thought for a moment. "You have to wonder what she's eating."

"Probably sardine-and-tomato-paste sandwiches, Mrs. Tranter," Susan said.

"Susan," her mother scolded, "don't be full of yourself."

"Oh that's all right, Cless," Mrs. Tranter said, smiling, studying Susan. "She's lovely enough to get away with it." Mrs. Tranter became thoughtful, then looked away. "I don't know," she said after a moment, "sometimes I think having my Etta here would be better than all the way up in Scotland."

The whistling of the bombs intensified.

"At least she's safe," Susan's mother said. "If Mac would let me, I'd send Susan here to my great uncle's brother-in-law's in—"

That's when these bombs hit *Poom! Poom!! Poom!!!* closer and closer until *BA-BA-BOOM!* The iron roof above them shook and groaned as if tearing, and the candle went black and the earth beneath the liner trembled and shifted with a turbulence so powerful that it actually lifted them and moved them about on the floor liner as if they were afloat, and then it quelled; the shocks, they quelled and became subdued and there was an incredible ringing in their ears that with their hands covering them in the pitch blackness they fought to muffle but could not.

Moments passed. The three of them suspended from sound and earthly sensation. Then the ground finally became reliable and familiar in its motionlessness and her mother called, "Susan? Susan?" through the settling din. "Susan!"

The darkness thick and absolute; no near-blindness this but blindness and its beyond.

"I'll—I'll get the candle," Mrs. Tranter said. "Wait. Here. Where? Oh God—God!"

"What?"

"The matches."

"Susan!" her mother called again.

"Yes—yes, Mum."

"For God's sake! Why didn't you answer?"

"I—I couldn't hear," she said. "I couldn't hear."

"The bloody matches," Mrs. Tranter said. "I can't find them. This is hell."

"Not quite yet," her mother said, "I've some—" The ringing went away enough for Susan to hear her mother grope for her purse, find it and snap open its clasp to then rummage. "Damn!" her mother said.

"I'll go up to the house," Susan said.

"No! No you won't," her mother said.

"I should go," Mrs. Tranter said. "After all—"

"No," her mother interrupted. "Don't you see? There is no house. We've been hit," she said. Her voice dropped to a whisper, yet one without a trace of self-pity: "Hit."

"You don't know that, Mum," Susan said. She crouched over as much as she could manage and stood and half-crawled to the corrugated shelter door. With some effort she pushed the door up and open and back.

With the City under complete blackout, in the dark October sky there was a breathtaking extravaganza of light and sound. Search lights swung and columned and skimmed the sky's dark and starry ceiling, slinging their beams back and forth, catching here and there an enemy wing, a tail, and the anti-aircraft guns would spark and punch blindly at it. The search lights all arced and pulsed and swung not as if they originated from the ground but as if they were tethered to the stars themselves and were hung in godly spectacle above both the Germans and the

English, both sides a rapt and willing audience. And of course there was the whistling of the bombs' descents and the *poom! poom!* when those whistlings died. And to the east, the mandarin glow of inexhaustible fires.

"Susan," her mother hissed. "Susan."

"It's like—like when they're on the trapeze," Susan said, "at the circus." She vaulted herself up and out and stood on the grass of the back garden. Ahead of her, through the totally black pitch of night, their house still stood. No more than a shadow but still standing. "It's not us, Mum," she called back down to the shelter. "Come see!"

"There!" Mrs. Tranter announced. "The matches!"

And Susan turned in time to see back down into the bunkered shelter as Mrs. Tranter struck a match and, cowling it with her hands, conveyed it to the candlestick. Light again filled the domed burrow and her mother came to the entranceway. "Who, then?" her mother asked.

"Ours, I should think," Mrs. Tranter declared.

Susan looked about. "It's not Mrs. Tranter's either," she told them.

"Alfred'll be pleased," Mrs. Tranter said, "if anything *could* please him."

Susan looked again at her house. Through the kitchen window she could see the faintest of glows, a soft yellow, and it seemed to move. "Mum?" she said.

"Yes, love?"

"Did you—"

"What?"

Her mother stood bent over down in the shelter's opening. The whistling descents of the bombs were more distant now and Susan began to walk through the encompassing darkness up the path and under the clothes line towards the house.

"What, love?" her mother called. "And where d'you think you're going?"

"Did you leave a candle on or anything?"

"No. And come back here. Susan!" her mother called in a loud whisper. "Susan!"

"There's a light on," she whispered loudly back to her mother. "In the kitchen."

She reached the window. There was a flower bed beneath it, the flowers now mere dark and petal-less stalks—no more flower-like than plumbing or wiring—and setting her hands on the windowsill she leaned across the flower bed and looked inside. That's when she realized there was no glass in the panes. Until this close, it had been too dark to notice. And there was the smell of smoke.

Again from the top of the bomb shelter her mother called with hushed stridency:

"Susan, come back here."

"There's smoke," she responded.

She went around the corner and tried the door. Its pane was gone too, cleanly as if it'd been removed by glaziers. She reached in and turned the dead bolt and pushed, and there was a scratching sound. That was the door brushing across the glass that her sandals crunched and crackled as she went in. A light, red and pointed, moved and flitted like a firefly over by the table.

"Hello?" she called. She stepped closer. Someone was there and it was her father. Just sitting there in the darkness, a cigarette burning in his hand. She could smell the half-wine half-whiskey smell of sherry and she said, "Dad?" He made no reply. He didn't smoke the cigarette, only held it. Then he sobbed. And her mother was at the back door with the candle.

"Mum," Susan said.

"The panes have all been blown out," her mother said. "Wait until your father gets home."

"Mum," Susan said again, "he *is* home."

Her mother entered, crushing with her shoes more glass. "Mac?" she asked Susan. "Where?"

Susan stepped aside and her mother came and stood by the table. The candlelight was tall and pale and the light leaned upon the wall and upon the ceiling and also too upon her father who was bent over now, his head in his hands, the smoke from his cigarette fluttering as it rose through the candlelight like a tiny scarf in a breeze. Her mother didn't say anything. She just set the candle on the table. By it was the sherry bottle and a glass and an ashtray and beside these scattered and everyday monuments was an envelope—yellow even in the candlelight with the wide stripe of blue reading PRIORITY—and beside it the telegram it had with scant ill earlier conveyed.

Her mother looked at these things—the bottle, the glass, the envelope—then stared at the telegram. Stared at her husband, her husband crippled with sorrow. "No, Mac," she said. "Don't, Mac—*please.*"

"Yes," he said, nodding, "yes."

"No, Mac," her mother said defiantly, "I won't hear it. I won't."

"It came to me at work," he said, his voice breaking.

"I won't hear it, I told you."

Susan picked the telegram up.

"I won't hear it," her mother said, desperately looking back and forth at the two of them, "won't hear it from either of you!"

Susan read, silently, and as word-for-word carefully as though bearing forth the decree of her *own* demise:

His Majesty's Government regrets to inform you that Flight Lieutenant Phillip Charles William . . .

"Put it down, Susan!" her mother demanded. She was shaking.

. . . Flight Lieutenant Phillip Charles William Mc-Ewan was reported missing. Our deepest . . .

"Please, Susan," her mother now pleaded softly, "put it down. Please?"

. . . reported missing. Our deepest sympathy.

"Down," her mother repeated to herself.

And then Mrs. Tranter was at the back door, asking:

"Are you all right, Cless? Cless? Susan?"

"Down."

Afterward

They let her take Phillip's final letter with her, and alone in the swaying compartment by the window she read it on the train. Eventually to Godmanchester. An evacuee. At Letchworth as the train chuffed in and idled in the station, a young man perhaps about Phillip's age strolled past on the platform, glanced in through the window, froze in mid-step, and opened the compartment door. She didn't look up. Just concentrated on the letter, conjuring forth her brother from within:

> *I'll be sending home soon another package of laundry, Mum.*

"Excuse me," the man said.

She looked up from the letter. His face was tanned, almost dark, like a character in the Bible, and he was finely dressed in a brown tailored suit. He carried a small suitcase and he wore a pair of white gloves and held a cane.

"D'you mind?" he enquired. An American accent. Like at the pictures.

"No," she said, "not at all."

"Good," he said, and he stepped in, and with that solid metal-and-leather *thoonk* of a train door he closed it behind him. With one hand he stowed his suitcase on the luggage rack above—opposite her—and he sat next to the window on the seat beneath, sat so gracefully that the movement might have been choreographed for him. He sleeked a cigarette case from his suit jacket's inside pocket and thumbing it open he offered her one.

"No, thanks," she said.

"Camels," he told her.

"Please, no."

She looked down at Phillip's letter. How—how could such an instrument still be? Still exist? Haunted and haunting calligraphy, each word utterly alive and inked in blue fountain pen on a tissue-thin aerogram. Shouldn't it have rightfully perished with him? Reside with him?

"It's okay, then?" the man asked.

She looked up.

"That I smoke?" he said.

"Yes, do."

Came a vague platform announcement about Peterborough.

"This is my only suit," he said.

"Oh." She didn't look up.

"Actually," he continued, "these are all the clothes I have in the world."

She didn't respond.

"My uncle gave it to me," he said. "The suit. As a favor to his brother. He's a tailor."

She thought for a second then looked up and nodded. "Yes," she said. She glanced up at his suitcase on the luggage rack above.

"Empty," he explained.

She blinked at him and returned her attention to the letter:

You'll be shocked to know, Mum, I've met a girl, Joyce, through Captain Grey of all people. You'll like her, Dad, quite good-looking, though Roger said not as pretty as our . . .

Her eyes skipped down a line or two until they touched on what she sought.

And Dad, please reconsider sending Susan up to Uncle Cec's brother-in-law. Ben, isn't it? The blacksmith? Look at it this way, Dad, not only will she be safe, but she might even learn a trade, ha, ha. (I know you're reading this, Susan, I do.)

She folded the letter over on itself, unable to continue. The conductor's whistle blew and the train lurched slightly and like all trains for an infinitesimal moment the linked carriages not only paused but almost reared back. Through the window, she could see the station building: dun-bricked, the mortar pock-holed from neglect, the pock-holes square, like a nag's missing teeth; the station's windows steamed and piped in peeling red. Slowly she shook her head.

"Everything going to be okay?" the well-dressed man asked.

"Who—who can say?" she answered.

Only now did the train couple forward, eventually clattering northward on its way.

POLO AT DAYBREAK;

OR, A PRAYER IN SNOWFALL

In the spring of 1982, at the age of thirty-one, Polo finally stared down the terror of being a grown-up. He chucked his job as a postman, wooed and courted a young emerald-eyed library student named Julie, and once they'd wed he installed them both in a renovated loft in Toronto's Beaches. Pleased with how effortless it seemed so far, he sprung for a fine-tailored pinstripe suit, a pair of gray flannel slacks, and a complementary navy blue blazer from The Brick Shirt House, each and all perfect for his new job at *Toronto Life* magazine hawking advertising space to restaurants. True, selling daunted him at first as he gathered his contacts and assembled a client list. But he reveled in both his sense of freedom and the admittedly hazy and romantic notion that he too was engaged in the free-enterprise adventure. His recently converted neo-Reaganite male friends however deemed it all amusing and gently taunted him that this very same romanticism had prompted him to vote for Olga Dobosh, Marxist-Leninist candidate for the riding of York-Scarborough in the 1974 federal election.

"Along with 160 other dreamers," he would remind them. "Besides, to paraphrase Karl himself, as a capitalist I'll be able to sell myself the very rope I hang me with."

Either way, this same wistful romanticism likely blinded him from all the warning signals. For in fact the economy had begun to falter even before he left the post office. And as interest rates soared past 20 percent during the summer of '82, the country caved into the pit of the worst recession since the 1930s. In Toronto alone hundreds of businesses went bankrupt every month. Many were restaurants. Polo's commissions abruptly leveled off then plummeted. When, as the junior rep, he was declared redundant the Friday before Labor Day, all he could do in his shock was wonder out loud to his embarrassed boss why people were always let go on Fridays.

Things worsened. He moped through the classified section all fall, one eye on the painfully thinning want ads, the other on their painfully thinning savings account. Desperate, Polo answered an ad in *The Globe and Mail* to work for the newspaper's circulation department. He donned his blazer and gray flannels, single-Windsor'd his red silk necktie beneath his shirt collar, and drove to the newspaper's district office above a 7-Eleven in Leaside.

"Bloody hell!" the district manager said. "We don't get many dressed like you." He boasted forearms as thick as barrels and wore a rubber apron knotted around the girth of an executioner.

"Er, what exactly will I be doing?" Polo asked.

"Newspapers."

"Ah—?"

"Four hundred and twenty-seven of the buggers."

"*Four* hundred?"

"And twenty-seven," the district manager said. "Delivering'm. Every morning. To the posh shites in Forest Hills."

Polo took it—what else could he do?—and thus an unemployed former postman with an anthropology degree found tentative rebirth—*tentative* rebirth—as a thirty-one-year-old paperboy.

Now Polo was a fussy man, and to ease the ordeal of delivering over four hundred newspapers six mornings a week, he quickly transformed it into ritual. He would inch out of bed at 3:45 a.m., shave, nuke some Sanka, pour apple juice instead of milk on his Cheerios, swallow his Vitamin C capsule, kiss Julie silently on the forehead, then scarper across the sleeping city to his eleven bundles of newspapers. To deliver them, he slung two canvas satchels around his shoulders like bandoleers and crammed each equally to the point of bursting.

Thus balanced, he hustled through his route, learning to roll and rubberband each paper without slowing his gait. When it rained or snowed, he slid the rolled-up newspaper cylinders inside special plastic bags, tucking the ends in as fastidiously as an apothecary at his calling. He earned $400 a week for the three grueling hours each morning, and because all his customers were billed quarterly by the newspaper he was spared the hassle of collections. Often he landed back home by seven thirty, his days each his own and in their entirety, hours passed with his books and vinyl—*Ulysses* and Merle Haggard, *The Day of the Jackal* and Vivaldi. From a Church Street pawn he ransacked a used video player—a Betamax of course—and on occasion watched his late father's favorite: Sergio Leone's *Once Upon a Time in the West*. But books had always been Polo's "high Mead," and browsing the Queen Street used bookstores one day he encountered Robert Aitken's *Taking the Path of Zen*. Truth be told, the only bits of "Zen" wisdom Polo had gathered had accrued from the TV beatnik Maynard G. Krebs, but for some God-only-knows reason Polo picked the book up and paged through it: "Cushions," "The Posture," "The Legs." He considered the book's weight—literally as well as figuratively. "CHAPTER ONE: FUNDAMENTALS: Accepting the Self." Hmm, maybe not—at least not today. But before he returned the book to its place Polo chanced a quick look at the dust-jacket photo of the author: the face, with its dark swept-back hair and clear eyes, was in every way a shiver-giver: a distinct and eerie resemblance to his late father—almost too much so. Still, thus did he procession it to the register and thence to home.

NEAR NOON THAT MORNING WHEN Julie returned from class, she noticed the book and asked him with a smile, "Finally teaching yourself to sit still?"

"And teaching myself to cook," he answered.

"I'll bring you home some donated *Bon Appétit*s," she told him.

Yet, too bashful to have Julie find him with a bona fide zafu, he improvised with one of the spare bed pillows, doubling the pillow over in its cotton case and then tucking it under his backside as he sat astride it. He'd face the wall and begin by counting his breaths, but he'd invariably end up by chasing his thoughts: veal Marsala; white lasagna with Parmigiano; chicken with prosciutto, fresh rosemary and pinot gris. When Julie gently teased him about the narrow regionalism of his recipe selection he responded with:

"What do you expect from a guy named Polo?"

"Nonsense," she laughed. "Your ancestors fought alongside Harold at the Battle of Hastings."

"They were Italian mercenaries," he countered back.

"That's not what your father told me," she said, poking out her tongue and silencing him.

WHAT ELSE HAD HIS FATHER told her? he wondered the next morning as he trudged up Forest Hills Road and wondered again later on his homemade zafu after he'd lost count of his breaths. And why all the incessant wondering? Frustrated by his lack of progress at this sitting business, he attempted to corral his thoughts in a journal. After all, hadn't Zen Roshi Aitken written a book? But what would he, Zen novice Polo, write in his own?

"Take the Zen guy's counsel," Julie suggested. When he looked puzzled, she added, "Pay attention. To your surroundings."

Of course. In the mornings. On his route:

03 *April 1983: The ground is ripe at sunrise. This morning I watched my shadow being born. Am getting better at one foot in front of the other.*

When Julie chanced upon it, she said, "Why Zandy, you're almost a poet."

They were standing by the sink in their kitchen. Quiet. Thoughtful. Through the bank of windows in the far wall of their Beaches' loft, they could see the roofs of their neighborhood descending gently to the lake, moored like rafts. Farther out, the darker blues of the motionless water and the softer blues of the sky above.

"I'm *almost* a lot of things," he said after a moment.

"For now," she said. Then added: "Be patient."

That spring, with the economy beginning to recover, Julie graduated. Not only did she get quickly placed with the City Library but she earned assignation to the lovely old branch by the lake. She bought a basal thermometer and secreted it under her pillow. One brilliant May morning she remained asleep until Polo came home. In stockinged feet he crept across the modest expanse of the loft and sat slowly on their futon's edge. She stirred and turned, opening her lovely green eyes and tickling back her dark bangs with her fingers.

"Feeling okay?" he asked. He touched her bare shoulder. She covered his hand with hers.

"Feeling like making a childe, actually," she answered, pronouncing the *e*. "You have plans?"

"Only those that match yours."

They made love slowly and at length, and lying in his arms afterward she held on to him with the intensity of a maiden. And when fourteen days later almost to the minute he returned home to the loft from his rounds, he again found himself un-alone: except this time instead of Julie on the futon, he con-fronted a near nativity of gifts: in the far corner where in meditation he sat and as if placed there by the magi themselves: a round pillow and no makeshift zafu this but a cotton-stuffed and brown-covered disc, one befitting the backside of a far less flawed aspirant than he but one he would struggle on none-theless. Atop it, a copy of *A Zen Wave: Basho's Haiku and Zen* by "the Zen guy," his adopted Roshi, Robert Aitken. And atop that? The best of all: a folded card of vellum parchment in-side which revealed a note, writ in hand and in fountain ink of deepest blue:

For my poet. No longer an almost.

At first, when the druggist confirmed Julie was pregnant, Polo was ecstatic. Indeed. For, see him now: racing through his papers, a newborn spring in his gait. He is whistling softly and arguing with himself over names: Leif, Tonya, Eveline, Gareth, Shoshanna, Bjorn, settling on Shoshanna. See him next borrowing Roger Tory Peterson's *Field Guide* from the library and searching the Church Street pawnshops for a pair of Zeiss Ikon binoculars. Though he'd be the first to admit he couldn't tell a swift from a swallow, he dares to plan birding hikes with his daughter in Glacier National Park in Montana, near where his in-laws summer. Shoshe—Shoshanna—would write A-grade essays about these wholesome vacations. He can see her beautiful scrubbed face in a class rowed with lesser children, her hand raised for every answer. Alas, it is precisely one of these vivid daydreams that breaks his easy cheerfulness and plagues him with self-doubt.

It happened on an unlikely morning in late November—a

crisp night draining off into an orange dawn, warm and still. Julie was at the cusp of her third trimester, making the child due right around Polo's father's birthday, the last week in February. He had finished the reno'd brownstones and was dogging it along St. Alban's when he imagined Shoshe in front of her sixth-grade class delivering an oral composition on her father:

"My dad's a paperboy," Shoshanna says, and the boys snicker.

"That's enough," snaps Miss Skittle. "She means her father works for the newspaper, as a reporter or something."

"No, Miss," Shoshanna says. "I mean he delivers the newspapers." All the kids laugh now.

"Every morning," Shoshanna continues, wounded but defiant. The laughter builds. Miss Skittle tries to hush them.

"Except Sundays," Shoshanna says lamely.

"No!" Polo shouted, shattering his reverie. He stared in horror at the rolled newspaper in his hand. On impulse, he pivoted and hurled the thing over the telephone wires. Then he drove straight home, remembering the conversation he'd had with his grandmother last Christmas, only now cast in a different light:

"You're as daft as your father," she had said.

"Daft?"

"Yes: always fretting about following your heart." She'd stood her sherry glass on the fireplace mantel and lit a cigarette and turned to Julie seated by the terrarium and added: "He watches far too much public television."

"We don't have television, Mrs. Bouton."

"Reba, Reba." She'd sighed. "And now this Hare Krishna

business." She'd shaken her head and taken a drag of her cigarette and continued: "You're not getting any younger," she had told him. "Scrap all this nonsense, move down here, and work for me. The market's booming. You could make fifty thousand selling condos and never even get your toe rubbers wet."

She lived in North Hatley, Quebec, drove a metallic-blue Trans Am, a widow who still used her toast rack and spoke doughboy French. Now, as soon as he got home he phoned her. Her machine answered. "Hi," the message began, "you've reached the home of Reba Bouton, Century 21's numero uno in the Eastern Townships."

Polo waited for the beep then left a short message. "This is your grandson Alexander. I'm coming to visit."

The day they left, Julie had a ten o'clock checkup at the obstetrician to see if the baby was still the wrong way around. The Toyota was packed, and Polo waited in the car, slouched in his seat and weighing the omens: it was December the 7th, the day before the Buddha's enlightenment—good—but also the day of Pearl Harbor—not so good. He attempted a read in Julie's Beryl Markham—*West with the Night*—but he quickly lost his concentration. For he was headed east—east with the morning. To Quebec, to his grandmother's, to dry-toe rubbers, to cold toast. Jesus H. Still, as Julie had said, it was only a visit. He didn't have to decide right away.

Finally Julie emerged from the doctor's, her shoulders slumped. She ran to the car, her parka clutched tight at the collar and across her swollen abdomen. She looked stricken and her pretty face twisted in worry.

"It's no different," she groaned. Now Polo could see she'd been crying. "Unless he can turn the baby around, I'll have to have a Caesarean."

It took Polo two hours until Belleville to distract her out of her grim mood. There were plusses, he pointed out. They could choose the birth date. And if she wanted, he could still be in the delivery room. They were so busy talking that he failed to heed the wind that punched in off Lake Ontario and knocked husks of snow across the highway. Near Kingston—about half-way to the Quebec border—the sky sagged and darkened and a steady snow started. The snow quickened with each exit they passed and Polo flipped the radio onto AM for the weather. By the cutoff for downtown Kingston, they were crawling through a nasty blizzard.

Suddenly in the road ahead a snow-sheeted policeman loomed, waving a spitting orange flare. "Take the exit!" he boomed. In the median a tractor trailer lay belly up like a fro-zen locust, its cab spavined. Other cars, maybe a half dozen broken and abandoned ones, pointed in every direction like the arms of slain compasses. Dead ahead, twin wrecks stared blankly at him, blocking the road, their side windows in a spi-derweb of shatters. "Exit now!" the cop commanded.

He did so. Unfortunately he was about six hundred and six-teenth in a line of cars queued up at the ramp's stop sign, all waiting to turn south in seek of the safe haven of Kingston Harbour.

"Maybe there's a power outage," Julie said.

"Maybe? We'll spend hours finding a room."

The queue advanced a space.

"Jesus," Polo said.

"Go the other way then," Julie suggested.

"Back?"

"North. The storms are always much worse by the lake."

"Really?"

"I'm a librarian."

"Right."

He eased the car out of the lineup, and half on the left soft-shoulder he squeezed past the queue to the stop sign and turned north. Almost at once the traffic thinned and they were alone on the road. As they sped through the countryside, the landscape flew past in snow-covered patches—as though each dormant pasturage was ripped by the wind from the earth's very crust. The road itself dipped and rolled, barreling through a barren world. They swept by a brown-bricked elementary school, its empty swings oscillating in the wind. They encountered a disbanded Shell station and then a low-slung motel built in the shape of a horseshoe. Indeed, that was what it was called. Beneath the HORSESHOE sign, only the red fluorescent No in the No VACANCY pulsed.

They pushed on. Night arrived as if it had spent the day crouched in the back seat. With the aid of her portable Book-lite, Julie read in her Beryl Markham and napped. Polo slowed at another motel but it had sheets of plywood battened across the windows. A third appeared to still be in business though the parking lot held scarce cars. Julie woke from the need to use the bathroom and he pulled in and drove up as close as he could to the office door. Julie hauled her legs out of the seat, and bent over in mini-steps she hurried the few feet to relief.

Hmm. He still though had his doubts about the place. Came a steady *whump-whump-whump*. Polo glanced in the rearview mirror then turned to fully apprehend the desolation of it all. Near the far end of the motel's single wing, the door to one room had been blown open, and the wind was repeatedly and mercilessly slamming the door open and shut, open and shut. When Julie came out of the office, her shoulders hunched up against her ears and shaking her head no, Polo offered no argument.

EVENTUALLY, THEY JUNCTIONED ONTO THE Trans-Canada. By nine thirty they reached Ottawa. Starved, they tracked down a Casey's Road House and stuffed themselves on chicken wings, Julie breaking her seven-month abstinence with a shandy. Polo borrowed the bartender's phone book and in the Yellow Pages discovered a hotel actually called The Talisman. The Talisman. How could a bloke like Polo not be drawn to such a name?

AS POLO COMPLETED THE CHECK-IN card, Julie yawned. The desk clerk, a baggy-faced young man, followed with his own.

"Sorry," the desk clerk said.

"Long day?" Polo asked.

"Finals. An imprint of your card?"

"Here," Julie said. She flushed her wallet from her purse

and plucked out her Visa. (Polo had months since "drawn and quartered" his own plastic, as he dubbed the procedure.)

"I'm a one L," the clerk told Julie. "In common law."

Julie yawned yet again. The clerk fought back his own and, victorious at least for now, processed her card. Polo hoisted their single bag, and in their room, he unpacked their clothing into the chest of drawers and listened to Julie scrubbing off her makeup and brushing her teeth in the bathroom. She emerged, raw-eyed, and sat in the bed and stuffed her legs under the covers.

"We're only staying a night," she pointed out.

"Sorry?"

"Why are you unpacking?"

He didn't know. He went and sat on the bedside, facing her.

"You all right?" he asked her before she could ask him.

"Uh-huh."

"Me," he confessed, "I'm still in the car."

She fooped back on the pillow and he tucked the covers around the swelling of their child. She closed her eyes and her face eased and softened with beauty. He stared across the room at the dense pleats of the drapes.

"Maybe *I* should go to law school," he said out of nowhere.

"*Un*-common law," she mumbled.

"I was being serious."

"I know."

She squeezed his hand in hers and when he turned he instantly read his face.

"It's enough that you'll love him," she said.

"I used to think so. Besides," he said, "it's a her."

"No difference to me."

Polo nodded.

"Other than the obvious," she added.

"Other than," he conceded. He sculpted the blankets around her head.

"But there is to you," she persisted. "A difference. Right?"

"Go to sleep."

"Right?"

"Sleep."

"Tell me."

"Yes," he admitted.

"How?" she asked. "How?" Reflexively she squirmed deeper under the blankets as if retreating, sorry she'd brought the subject up.

"With boys," he said, "you don't have to worry about a son-in-law."

"My folks don't," she said. "Though you won't believe me."

"You're right," he said, "I don't believe you." In response she frowned, but he bowed his head and lowered his lips to her eyes and kissed them closed.

"Go have a nightcap," she told him, her voice muffled by the blankets. "Or two. Nothing will happen tonight."

He stood.

"Sure?"

"Yes."

At the door he flicked off the light. He waited. Waited for her to say yes again, but she didn't.

•

HE RODE THE ELEVATOR TO the rooftop lounge. There, four men had gathered on bar stools around a grand piano drinking and laughing. Behind them was a plate glass window and beyond it the winter storm still howled through the skyline, streaking the night with contrails of snow.

Polo shivered and claimed the last stool. The singer was obviously on break and he pivoted and searched for a waitress.

"You're best to fetch it yourself," said the man on Polo's right. The man tilted his pipe in the ashtray and smoothed his military crew cut.

A few minutes later Polo capitulated though he wandered around the entire lounge before finding the bar. There, a slick-suited man stood to the side working his jawbone. A woman Polo guessed to be the singer was talking at him. The man waved his hand through the smoking air for silence.

"So what d'you want me to do," he said loudly to her, "change the goddamn weather? We got customers."

"Why do I bother?" said the singer. She rolled her eyes at Polo and stamped off.

"Women!" the man said to Polo, skirting around behind the bar. "You married?"

"And pregnant," Polo answered.

"Jesus," the man said. "Stump city."

"What?"

"Nothing," the man said. "So what's yer other poison?"

Back at the piano, the singer, now seated, smiled at Polo. He coastered his Stroh's in front of his stool and she rolled her eyes again as he sat down. "Hi. I'm Kathy, the singer," she said. She muted the microphone with her covering hand. "And that," she said, "was Theo, the shit."

She asked Polo his name and where he was headed.

"We got caught in the storm," he answered.

"We?"

He nodded. "My wife Julie's down in our room, sleeping."

"Tired?" asked Kathy.

"And seven months pregnant."

"That's pregnant," Kathy said.

The military guy beside Polo said, "Hear! Hear!" He raised a toast to mothers and babies, and everyone drank, and then Kathy played. She sang the standards—"New York, New York," "Hey Jude"—but did so in a clear if narrow voice, and two or three of the drinkers crooned along over the refrains. Not Polo however. After several songs a waitress came by and everyone ordered another round. One man stood Kathy a Baileys. He wore a wide orange tie with a green cartoon cobra in sunglasses painted on it. He caught Polo staring.

"My kid, he entered this in the Father's Day ugly tie contest," the man said through his French accent. "It took second place."

"One more song and I'm going home to my little boy," Kathy announced.

"Willie Nelson," Polo suggested, the beers gentling his innate shyness. "'My Heroes Have Always Been Cowboys.'"

"Ah, country," Kathy said. "A man after my own heart. Only I don't know *that* one well enough. You come sing it."

Everyone cheered.

"Er, I'd rather not," Polo said, and everyone booed. He thought of his other country favorite. "'Stand By Your Man,' then?"

Silence. Kathy took a moment.

"I—I can't," she said.

"But—why not?" he asked.

She shrugged and looked away. "Why else?" she answered, and with these words her voice faltered. She returned her attention to her piano's keyboard, her fingers gliding up and down the keys though her fingers brought forth no music. Polo looked about, looked at the men hunched forward and leaning on their elbows. All of them toyed with their empty glasses and avoided his eyes. Then he knew. Crap! Was he that bloody insensitive? *Stand By Your Man?* *I can't.* *Why not?* Huh: *Why not?*

Then the Quebecois coughed and said to Polo in a low voice, "Her garçon left her, left her the day she had her kid. Tabernac, eh? Hasn't sung it since."

Polo stared at the guy in disbelief. Jesus. The same day? "Tabernac indeed," was all he managed.

"Oui," the Quebecois agreed.

For a moment Polo gathered his nerve. He exhaled.

"Look," he said to Kathy, "I—I'm sorry."

"Don't be," she said. "None of it's *your* fault."

"I don't know," he said. "Guilt by gender?"

She laughed and her fingers stilled on the keyboard and she studied him for a moment.

"Seven months?" she asked him.

"Yes."

"And she's down there in your hotel room?"

"Yes. Sleeping."

She thought for a second. "Tell you what," she said. "You do Willie, and I'll do Tammy."

"Wait," he objected. "Listen—"

"Deal?"

He looked around. The other choristers all nodded their heads at him.

He sighed. "Deal," he said, and he gulped his beer for false courage but in that moment Kathy had already begun and from some far-away locked-up place she sang:

Sometimes it's hard to be a woman . . .

They let her sing it alone. Came Polo's turn. He cadged the Quebecois's ugly tie and looped it bandanna-style around his head and knotted it at his nape, careful to tuck it in behind his ears.

"He looks just like him," the Quebecois quipped to the army guy, and Kathy swung the mike over by its boom and she played the opening bars and at her cue Polo summoned forth whatever hangdog sadness lurked in his heart and he sang:

I grew up dreamin'
of bein' a cowboy
and lovin' a cowboy's ways.

His voice broke twice but he nailed every single word and at the end everyone clapped and cheered, even Kathy. Polo's face reddened and in a single swallow he chugged the remains of his beer. Then he helped Kathy stow her gear.

"Good luck," he said.

"You too."

He returned the tie and succumbed to another Stroh's. He sat talking until the bar closed then elevatored down to his room.

WHEN HE SHUT THE DOOR behind him, the room vanished into the pitch darkness. He smelled the fust of the used furniture and the lemon of the rug deodorant and he heard Julie snoring faintly. He sidestepped into the bathroom and grappled for the light switch. He ran the tap and forced two glasses of tepid water down his throat. He doused the light and carried a third back into the room. With his thigh he nudged his way past the foot of the bed and flopped into one of the leatherette chairs by the drapes. He stared until Julie's outline became flesh in the blackness. He somehow managed the last glass of water and stood the empty on the floor. Then he promptly passed out.

The crick in his neck and the dry heat hauled him awake three hours later. Sweat mortared his shirt against his back, and his trousers bunched like cordage behind his knees. He struggled aright in the darkness, groping to remember just where he was. Road terror, the other magazine salesmen had termed it. But before he could panic, he heard Julie's voice in his mind: *Pay attention—to your surroundings.*

Yes. Yes, indeed. So he stood and fumbled with the radiator buttons for the "off" position and he peered out through the drapes but a patina of rime obscured any view the glass door might've afforded. So he slid open the door and sidestepped out onto the balcony, ducking first under the dangling stilettoes of the icicles. Outside, the world that braced him was still and cold, and sweet with the scent of cedar, and flakes of snow as big as mushrooms filtered down from the purple sky.

Beneath that sky, Ottawa spread east, rising in soft glittering folds and Polo stood there at the balcony's railing and looked outward thinking, It's only four thirty, but already life's afoot in this tidy city. Roll-your-own men delivering vans of warm bread. Newspapers in plastic bags left in porch snow. He pictured all the paperboys unleashing bundles of newspapers, snapping the brittle wires. On a morning this cold he would jog to keep warm and by the end of his route he would be drenched with sweat as if riding herd. Out of nowhere a line came to him and he ached to write it down but his journal was at home in his desk. This void saddened him until shivering he knelt onto one knee and where the balcony met the railing he wrote with his finger in the furl of snow:

> *To ease your path*
> *I will gather*
> *a lariat of snowflakes*

He stopped writing. Did he need to write differently, upside-down or backwards perhaps, so that someone looking down from the stars could read it? He bent even closer to the ground until he could hear the snowflakes landing, the flakes quietly populating the snowdrift beside his ear. Curls of his breath swam and danced in the grooves that the letters had made in the snow and the cold veritably heaved all about him as though he temporarily inhabited a massive lung of ice. Yes. If I can understand it this close, you can understand it even from the farthest end of night and all time to come.

He arose and whapped the snow off his knees. He reclaimed his arms by stropping them with his hands through the thin cotton of his shirt. And then, oddly, he placed his palms together and very very slowly he bowed. Deeply. Bowed from the waist. "Oddly" because he had never ever done such a thing in his life.

Inside, the room had cooled and he blew into his cupped hands. His stomach grindled but the coffee shop didn't open for two hours. He would wait it out in bed. He peeled off his clothes and with the utmost care slid under the blankets and sheets. Julie was on her side, her legs tucked into themselves, her body face-away from his. He molded his upper body alongside her spine and he reached around and caressed her swollen tummy, in seek of the child within, and for no small time he lay there, lay there listening to his unborn daughter, listening to the seas and shores of her dreams.

As morning beckoned, he fell asleep.

THE HANDSOMEST
MAN, ON EARTH

Riordan had been dead barely a half hour when his cell phone rang. Damn, he cursed, I'll bet the afterlife has wicked roaming charges. In actuality, he stood in the shower, but as a freshman engineering student at Montana State University fifty years earlier, he'd been assigned Michel de Montaigne's "To Philosophize Is to Learn How to Die" in his sole English lit class and it had taken up immediate and permanent residence within his soul. And so now all these years past did he fumble in the stricture of his coffin for his phone—i.e., he stepped out of the shower and retrieved it from the bassinette.

"Hello?" he said.

"Dad?"

It was one of those new "smart" phones—a Nokia 7190—given on his retirement as a turn-of-the-millennium version of the gold watch.

"Dad? You there?"

"John?"

"Dad—Dad, I can't *believe* you're getting married today."

"Sorry?"

"You heard me."

He had heard—Jesus, but he had. Naked in the steam-swirling oppression of his bathroom, he bell-ringer'd a thick towel off the bathroom door rack, glancing in the medicine-cabinet mirror as he did.

"Well?" his son asked.

He crooked the phone between his shoulder and ear to free both his hands then wrapped and tied the thick flannel of the bath towel about his waist. Somewhere within the clouds of the medicine-cabinet mirror he scruffled his fingers through his full head of rich gray hair until it was an unkempt mess. He wanted to mug (he could manage a Palme d'Or Jagger) but thought the better of it.

"Dad," his son said, "I mean, Christie—Christine— would've been forty-one today."

He sighed. Then cursed, silently.

"Forty-one," his son repeated. "Today."

He counted to ten: one, two, three . . . , then said softly:

"You think I don't know that?"

It was getting suffocating in the bathroom—as if he'd been reincarnated as the whistle in the devil's teakettle. He yanked open the bathroom door.

"I'm not saying you don't know," his son upbraided him. "I'm simply pointing out that you're acting *as if* you don't know. What if Mom finds out?"

This absurdity brought him back to earth: their hallway.

"What?"

"You heard me. What if Mom finds out?"

"In the priory?"

"She could."

"They have AOL after Matins?"

"This *is* the twenty-first century."

"Barely. Christ, Son, they're nuns—cloistered nuns. They probably don't even know fucking Kennedy's dead."

"Shite!" his son said.

His phone—perhaps indeed "smart" but a fob'd watch nonetheless—read, CALL ENDED.

RIORDAN'S GIVEN NAME WAS JONATHAN, "Jack," and women loved him. All women. Didn't matter what. He'd be in the deli of the Safeway and some woman waiting beside him for her order of Black Forest ham would peer into his shopping basket and then look up at him, her eyes caressing his face, and say, I've never tried Bleach Wipes, and he'd reply, Neither have I. When he was a kid, one day he'd gotten a flat tire on his coaster bike (this was centuries ago, mind you), and this really, *really* pretty older woman (i.e., in her twenties), pulled her Buick Roadmaster (or was it an Olds Ninety-Eight?) over to the side of the road and asked him if he needed any assistance. He was eleven. Or thirteen maybe. He couldn't remember. But she had drawn-back hair the color of ripe strawberries, and a white cotton blouse as packed and promising as twin pomegranates. When she bent over in her pedal pushers to examine his tire, he became forever smitten by that part of the female anatomy: the dimple at the base of a woman's spine and what was foretold beneath.

OR MAYBE HE'D JUST IMAGINED that—the "older" woman in the pedal pushers. For what eleven-year-old boy (or even thirteen-year-old) would compare a woman's breasts to pomegranates? Perhaps he might've. You see, he was the oddest of ducks, our Jack Riordan. Now, as he stood in their bedroom in front of the mirror detangling his hair with Bea's hairbrush, he thought for the countless time why he hated his good looks and why for the countless countless time he hated hating them. As per, he had not the faintest clue. It had always been thus. Now, done with his hair, he slipped out of his bath towel and draped it over the brass rail of their king-sized bed. He pulled on his underwear (Hanes white jockeys) and a pair of black Dockers socks. He and Bea had agreed to do this wedding bit semi-casual (after all, they'd lived together for 11 years and 3.5 months, so why not?). In their walk-in closet, he took a pair of charcoal chinos off the hanger then engaged in a spirited debate with his shirts and ties.

"You're not going to choose me, are you?" the most brazen of his shirts asked him.

"You're pink," he pointed out.

"Bea bought you me for your birthday."

"Yes, and I wore you."

"To clean out the garage."

"Consider yourself lucky. The septic tank's pending. Any hands up?"

But then he softened and lifted the pink's sleeve, caressing it. She had indeed bought it for his birthday—100 percent broadcloth cotton, hand-stitched with sleeve-cuff slits for cuff links (Bea thought buttoned shirt-cuffs to be charmless). He weighed his options. Here he was: until this very morning, a guy who had toiled for four decades for Burlington Northern and then for Montana Rail Link, four decades devoted to walking the lines inspecting the rails and ties of the rail bed, the stiles and traves of the trestles beneath—inspecting them for faults and fractures of stress—could that guy get married in—in pink?

"You could wear the lavender tie," the pink suggested.

"Or I could strangle you with it."

"No you won't," it told him. "Not on this day."

"God, Jack," Bea squealed when he got out of the cab at the courthouse curbside. "You look like the marquis of Avingdon," she said, impishly pronouncing it "mar-kwiss."

"Who?"

He ducked his head back into the cab and paid the driver— Five, ten; here, keep it; thanks, pal. Behind him waited the courthouse pillars and steps and towering above them the building's dome, white and glittering in the early September sunshine. Perched atop that dome stood a square white cupola, missing only an enigmatic lighthouse widow to inhabit it and grant it perfection.

"Beautiful day for it," Bea said, extending her hand towards him as if he might deign it with a kiss. Instead he took her hand and her other in his and now as always marveled at them. Only a desperate suitor would describe Bea's hands as delicate. They were too large; but with the slenderness of her fingers, those hands exuded an aura of both fragility and strength. Besides, while ever her suitor, on this his wedding day he was no longer quite as desperate.

He kissed her cheek.

"Now you've really guaranteed our having bad luck," she pronounced.

He shrugged a shoulder and in that lambent curbside sunlight executed a half step back and surveilled this marvel to which he had committed everything and all: her shortish auburn hair that she had colored from gray and swept back from her face in layers and waves; she wore a cream-colored V-necked dress of either chiffon or silk, its blouson close-fit and only partially camouflaged by a Belgian cotton blazer. A large matching purse was slung over one shoulder and her high-heeled open-toed shoes rendered her legs more teenaged than they had been in decades.

"You're almost tall in those," he said.

"Not if you subtract the mousse and styling gel," she countered. She smiled, her large brown eyes crinkling.

"Well, either way, you look positively beautiful," he said.

"I look like my father," she said. She let go of his hands and unclasped her purse, opening it and prospecting inside as though it were someone else's—a dear aunt's perhaps, who'd requested her young niece to fetch her cigarettes, or rather her wallet that she might even up with the pharmacy delivery boy.

"I—I bought you a wedding present," Bea said. "Two, actually, though one's intangible."

"One's what?"

Now, curbside in the street the taxi revved, and its transmission clunked into drive, and it lurched out incautiously into the Broadway traffic. Horns screeched and brayed.

Bea scowled at the driver and clasped shut her purse. She tugged at Riordan's arm. "Come on," she said cheerfully, leading him up the path towards the courthouse steps. "This is no place for any exchange of gifts."

They walked hand in hand, her heels a rhythmic copa on the dry-set pavers. When they walked like this, as though led by a horse-drawn chaperone through the emerald hills of Kerry or Connaught, Bea swung their joined arms in exaggerated cadence to her footsteps: a girlish affectation, Riordan thought, its incongruity all the more endearing. On the ample lawn to one side, a mime troupe, the blanched fard already applied to their faces, was setting up chairs in the manicured grass for the lunch-hour performance. Today a mime. Tomorrow perhaps puppet theatre. Each and all gratis of course. Once, while meeting Bea here for a hurried finger lunch (her city hall office was housed in the courthouse annex), Riordan had been transported back to his childhood by a performance of a one-man band. That fellow however hadn't performed the "Roll Out the Barrel"s or "Knees Up Mother Brown"s that Riordan anticipated but, instead, selections from Vivaldi's *Four Seasons*, the allegro from Mozart's Piano Concerto in D Minor, and the "Valse" from Tchaikovsky's *Sleeping Beauty*. The fellow played at once a clarinet and a cello and a tympani and too a strange clavicle that looked like a large cricket bat replete with piano wires and keys.

Lost, Riordan was, in this reverie, at least until they reached the courthouse steps. There he found himself perspiring, and not just from the midday warmth that encased them like a humidor, but from his nervousness. Indeed, he found himself slightly embarrassed by such trepidation. He was just another old geez, as his dad would've said, a dapper one to be sure, but an old geez nonetheless. Summoning forth a not-entirely false vein of bravura, he again sought both Bea's hands and they faced each other as if to rehearse the very vows they were in minutes scheduled to utter.

Then an errant thought came, apropos of nothing, and with that thought a look of mild puzzlement.

"What?" Bea asked.

"Who's—who's the marquis of Avingdon?" he asked her.

"Who?" She searched his face.

"The marquis of Avingdon. You said I looked like him when I got out of the taxi."

Bea laughed. "I haven't the faintest," she confessed. "Just a name that popped into my head to, I don't know, summate the regalness of your arrival."

"Regalness? In a Yellow Cab?"

Again she laughed. "Your appearance," she said. "You know, how you're dressed."

"You bought me this shirt. This tie."

"Jack," she said. "It was nothing. Just a name. Maybe I heard it years or ages back. What does it matter, hmn? Now come on," she scolded him, prompting him up the courthouse steps. "I've a meeting in an hour and I want to give you your wedding present."

IT WAS A '96 NEWMAR Mountain Aire—his present for Bea—the DiMaggio of motor coaches, but it had been, according to the salesman's phraseology, "Tits-to-toe custom built"; and was it so: a gorgeous dual-axel'd forty-foot road cruiser with a king-sized bed and knock-outs for the kitchen and living room. It had a mere twenty-five-thousand-odd miles and sure it cost him a spendy $125K but this was for Bea—for the two of them, actually—so cost be damned. It was bolted atop the incomparable Freightliner chassis and the coach itself was El Dorado silver with Barcelona-red flames and chevrons on its sides for eye appeal and a Cummins 450 horsepower diesel behind the rear bulkhead for guy appeal. As for the interior décor, that boasted a blend of soft rose-petal hues—neither true pinks nor rich reds. These colors owned shades more shy, more demure. But what Riordan really liked above all was the genuine leather of the seats up front, the same soft succulent fine-grain leather that Formula One drivers supposedly wore on their hands when they maneuvered their own motorcars; except these twin seats, as beckoning as an after-date couch, were ones earmarked for the mister and missus—at least Riordan both hoped and supposed. Back outside in the sales yard though, during the ceremonial tire-kick, he hesitated when he remembered his late younger brother Robert, feeling a bit sheepish about the garish chrome that glittered on the wheels and bumpers, on the grille and the rocker panels.

"If it don't go, chrome it," he had muttered to himself.

"Say again?" the salesman had asked.

The RV dealership stood out on the dry heat mirage of the Clark Fork flats—on the way west out of town, just adjacent to the newly reno'd international airport.

"Something my kid brother used to say," Riordan told him.

At a far distance on the cloudless horizon, the Bitterroot Range towered and sparkled, blue-greens and granite. In this blinding whiteness of sunlight, Riordan wandered around to inspect the back fenders and bumper. The salesman tagged a step behind. On the back fender was mounted the spare tire, encased in a glinting disc of steel. More chrome. Way more painfully glittering chrome. Riordan took a moment's moment. Chrome. Yeah, well, Rob, it won't be your brass, right?—your ninety-six thou. As Riordan chewed on this bittersweet veritas, he noticed the license plates: blue numberings on a background of crisp whiteness. A vaguely British flag in the plate's dead center between the three letters and the three subsequent numbers. All framed by an upper silhouette of a mountain range's peaks.

"Kanuckistanis," the salesman had said. "BC-ers." The salesman had chewed at the inside of his cheek before plunging on. "Have to tell ya, older couple, twin suicides. The previous owners. Harmless enough. No blood. No mess at all."

Riordan faced the man. "Inside?"

"Sí. They'd donned those whatsits—you know, old duffers diapers."

Riordan had turned away, his eyes back on the motor coach but his sights far afield. Thus had he conjured the scene: the two old little dears, white-haired and beautiful. Dressed in identical hues and fabrics. The AC on. OxyCons to serenely OD on and bring down that quietest of curtains. Plain chant on the CD player. The two seated in the pilot's and co-pilot's seats. No, the old guy'd've let her drive—yes, he would've. Each reaching out for the other's hand: two beloveds, the final hand-hold but the most heartfelt and poignant of all gone before.

"Bit of a turn-off, right?" the salesman had said.

"Hmm? What?"

"A turn-off. Well?"

"I'll pay cash," Riordan had told him. "No dickering."

"We'll—we'll have to tidy it up first. Empty it. You know, of their cups and saucers."

"Don't bother. I want it as is. And I get to keep the license plates."

THE T-SHIRT HAD THICK ALTERNATING black and yellow horizontal stripes and was captioned *Killer Bea's*. Now that he'd unwrapped it, he held it up by its shoulders and at arm's length.

"What do you think?" Bea asked.

"Does it come with antennae?" Riordan quipped.

Bea cuffed him playfully across the shoulder. "Turn it around," she suggested. "Then it'll make sense."

By quickly crossing one forearm over the other, he did so. *"Bea Ireland, Independent, for County Commissioner,"* Riordan recited softly. He reread it, silently. "I—I don't get it," he said.

"What's not to get?" Bea asked.

He uncrossed his forearms and folded the T-shirt length-wise in half and looked at her. "The 'Independent' bit for one thing."

"How so?"

"How so? Bea, your father was the Woody Guthrie of hard-ware clerks. Inde*pen*dent?"

"Jack, the political climate is changing. I have to adapt."

"Adapt?"

"Okay, adjust. Reposition myself."

"Wait—wait a second; just a second," he said. "Adapt. Ad-just. Reposition. That's fine, but what about our plans?"

"Our plans."

"Yes. The Grand Canyon. Baja. Maccha—you know—"

"Picchu."

"Right. And Patagonia."

"Jack, Jack, those haven't changed. They're just—*I'm* just asking—asking you to put them on—on hold."

"On hold?"

"For a while."

"But we've been planning for months."

"I know. But—"

"And I bought you a—bought us—" He couldn't finish. He felt slightly dizzied.

"Just for a while," she said.

"A while?"

"Yes."

"A while. Oh, that's ripe. And what if you win?"

"I'm not going to win. Rumor has it that Metz is going to run as the Democrat."

"Bea, look at this." He unfolded and held up the T, the caption towards her: *Killer Bea's*. "Metz can run all he wants. You're going to win and . . ." His voice, chased by his self-pity, trailed off. He fell silent. She graced the back of his wrist with her fingertips. Then took his hand and gave it a squeeze.

"Come on. We can't keep the j.o.p. waiting."

He glanced at his watch: the hour had arrived. What to do? What to do? He felt as if the carpet—red and leading to the glorious premiere of their final act—had been yanked out from under him. On Broadway Avenue, Bea's surprise wedding present, the Mountain Aire motor coach and driven by the salesman himself, slowed and turned left, exactly as scheduled and destined for the lot behind the courthouse. Gift wrapped, in a way.

"Look," he said, flustered. "You—you go."

"Go where?"

"To—to your meeting."

"And?"

"I'll—I don't know. I'll see you later."

"Jack. Honey. You can't be serious. It's—it's a T-shirt, for Petey's sake. A T-shirt."

"Yes," he said. He attempted to give it back to her, but she held up her hands and stepped back. So he settled for a less-than-wry witticism: "And it does indeed have antennae," he said. "The reception? Loud and clear."

•

WITH HIS OWN SET OF keys, he steered the coach west along Broadway, the town's charm thinning noticeably. Past the city's limits, Broadway widened and offered ample soft shoulder, allowing him to pull over and continue in safety the conversations he thought he should've had with Bea. You know, those spot-on conversations in which we justify and validate our infantile behavior and vindicate our childish selfishness. To wit:

I mean, what if the roles were reversed?

Reversed?

Exactly. What if, I don't know, we had agreed—you and I had agreed, that you would indeed run for County Commish—

And?

And after you'd served, won and served, then *we would take off and be free.*

Jack, I don't know that logging a thousand miles a day is exactly freedom.

Will you let me finish, huh? Just once? Just this once?

DOING THUS WAS TIRESOME, so he took a breather and sank deeply into the soft leather of the driver's seat. With his hand, he stroked the gentle softness. Did they still tan leather? Strop it by hand? Or was it these days done by some insidious and insensate machinery? Well? Christ, who cared? Apparently, he did. If he continued he'd go mad—hell, he had gone mad! Enlisting the steering wheel as a fulcrum, he catapulted himself up out of his soft-leather cocoon and stood at the cusp of the coach's living quarters. To this side—the passenger's side—the kitchen countertops, the brushed-nickel faucet, matching taps and sink; the identical brushed-nickel four-door refrigerator: twin freezer doors above, twin reefer doors beneath. To the interior's other side—the driver's side—the round teak dining table then the rose-leather couch. The flat-screen TV, wall-mounted and diva-worthy. Beyond all this, the entrance to the shower, the lav, the loo. Not to mention the bedroom. Ah, yes: the honeymoon suite. The workbench, to which his father referred it. Emotionally drained by this catalogue of now-worthless assets (especially the last two items), Riordan plunked back down in the driver's seat and loped his legs out to the side, lanky as a ranch hand, though few if any ranch hands wore pink dress shirts and lavender ties to their nuptials. Of course, he hadn't partaken in any nuptials. For a second, he wondered what Bea was doing. Thinking of her rekindled his previously dispatched monologue with her:

As I was saying, what if we, the two of us, had agreed to see the world only after *you'd won and served?*

Go on.

And then, I don't know, as a wedding present I gave you a T-shirt that announced and listed Jack & Bea's World Tour starting not after *you won and served, but on* this *very day?*

She didn't answer. So he persisted:

Well? Well?

Still not answering. Damn it. But he had a point, hadn't he? Hadn't he?

"Aw, shite," he cursed. He struggled aright. Between the driver's and passenger's—the pilot's and co-pilot's—was the console, as tall and substantial as an ottoman and covered in the same exquisite "Formula One" leather. Riordan probed around just under the lip until he found the catch that released the lid. It yawned open smoothly and gradually, obviously as well-engineered as it was well-upholstered. As for what was revealed inside, that was a disparate trove of retro reading materials—Josephine Tey's *The Daughter of Time*, John Hersey's *Hiroshima*, and a soft-cover edition of Pablo Neruda's *Cien sonetos de amor*, the English translations by Stephen Tapscott. Jesus: love poems. Just what he needed.

But the console also yielded a stack of magazines, one as square-shouldered and presentable as a vestment. A tidy lot, these Canadians. Riordan perched on his seat's edge and sifted through them: *Time, Maclean's, Sunset.* Amongst these lay several issues of *Vancouver Life*, a glossy-covered mag that Riordan assumed was the Canadian version of *The New Yorker*. The issues were all dated in the late 1980s and early '90s but were devoid of dog-ears or vented spines. One, April 1989, was even sealed away in its own gallon-sized freezer bag. It proclaimed itself the "Getaway Issue" by heralding inside its cover *Planes & Boats & RV Trains*.

With the care of a curator, Riordan extracted it from its sealage and explored its pages: "For BC Ferries, The Sunshine Coast Reigns!"; "Boo-Hoo the Cariboo: The Loss of BC's Last Best Place"; "RV or YVR?: To Drive or Arrive." This latter story concerned itself with two writers' records of their respective journeys to Disney World—one by driving, the other by flying. Filler stuff, Riordan decided. Adequately written, but he could find no substance, no gravitas that might justify the seemingly hallowed status of this particular issue. But then, towards the end of the RV/YVR story, he uncovered said gravitas, contained in a two-page sidebar titled "Lunch, at the End of the Runway." Tucked in the pages' fold was a smaller plastic bag, sealed. Inside awaited three letters written on aerogram tissue—each as thin and sky-blue as butterfly wings—and accompanied by a poem in Spanish, a sonnet, transcribed via quill and inkwell and on the most exquisite of cloth vellums:

No te quiero . . .[7]

Gravitas. In both languages. Or any for that matter. Two lives' and three deaths' worth.

7. I do not love you . . .

At Whippoorwill Drive Riordan banked his craft hard left and piloted a near quarter mile, then slowed and stopped on this side of the fence opposite Runway #11. In the narrow roadway, he negotiated a two-point turn without the aid of tugboats or light sticks and backed into the ample shoulder which was a lamentable admix of gravel, dust, and whin. It was noon, an hour and an eternity since he'd broken with Bea. He sat in his captain's chair and drummed his fingers on the helm—okay, the steering wheel. Here he was at the end of the runway, and he wanted lunch. He unloped himself from behind the steering wheel and in the fridge was touched to find that the salesman had arranged a perfectly wondrous wedding present; for there on the shelf stood a startling and chilled oasis: two bottles of Taittinger Rosé—the legendary pinot noir/chardonnay blend. Beside the champagne waited two cut-crystal champagne flutes, each sheened with frost and the two standing like figurines on a wedding cake. And propped against the Taittinger's? The former owners' BC license plates: PNM 103.

> *But most haunting of all were Susan and Roger. Retired Brits who came here to the end of the runway every day, parked their RV at 11:09 a.m. precisely (7:09 p.m. Lockerbie time: the exact and harrowing hour and minute that the on-flight bomb exploded). They would then unfold Blackpool deck chairs on the grass and as the approaching 747s and L-1011s hooshed and floated above them, crisp and graceful as origami cranes, Susan and Roger would lunch here at the end of what was for them this saddest of all cafés.*

Now Riordan knew: Lockerbie, Scotland: Pan Am Flight 103.

THE SUN DOESN'T SET IN Montana, it dissolves, trying to both hasten and linger, like ice on the hood of a late-summer convertible. This breathless dissolution of the planet's sun is even more pronounced as the equinoxes approach, and on this day—the tenth day of the ninth month of the second year of the new millennium—the autumnal equinox was knocking with no small vigor at time's back door.

Knocking too was the captain of police, a fellow by the name of Robert Tully Sims. Except the door Captain Sims was knocking at was Riordan's RV door. Now, no cardboard-epaulet captain this; Captain Sims possessed ample bona fides: back in the woeful winter of '87, he'd shot and fatally wounded an AK-47-armed perpetrator outside the Wells Fargo branch by the mall, the parking lot ice splayed with a grotesque pie of purple-and-wheat-colored viscera; in the summer of '92, with a metal baseball bat, he single-handedly battered three members of the Los Angeles motorcycle lycanthropes The Mongols into surrendering while they were in the midst of methodically trashing the VFW bar on West Main, trashing it on the one night a week the VFW rented it out to the local gay community; not the least, to Captain Sims especially, he had authored and had published three well-received crime novels: *Baby-Blue Sky Blues*, *The Solid Gold Cadillac*, and *Reservations Are for Iridescents*—this final one translated into French of all things. A worthy adversary by any means even with this abridged laundry list. As for the captain's pedigree, he also could boast about that: he was Bea's son by her high school sweetheart. Out of wedlock. When she was barely fifteen.

"Jack? You in there?"

"Of course I'm in here. Who the fuck're you?"

"Bob. Er, Robert."

"The Dibbles?"

"That's us. Can I come in?"

"Nada. Get the fuck ta shite."

"Er, you're sounding more than a little Butte. Been drinking?"

"Champagne's not drinking."

"Jack, let me in, okay?"

"The door's not fucking locked."

"Jesus fucking-H."

"Leave Him out of this."

"I'm coming in."

"Hopefully not with your weapon drawn."

"Ha. I'm not even in uniform."

The captain entered, stepping up into the cockpit. Down and to the side, Riordan was comfortably sprawled at the oval dining room table, sizing the captain up. "You know," Riordan told the captain, "if you were any near tall, you'd be tall, dark, and handsome."

"Blame my mother."

"I do indeed. For everything."

The captain wore jeans and a plaid cotton shirt, the shirt unbuttoned at the collar and its vents untucked at the waist.

"Champers?" Riordan asked, gesturing to the half-empty second bottle on the table. These two Taittinger's were now kept company by three long-necked and very-drained Buds.

"What kind is it?"

"The champers?"

"Sí."

"Frog."

"Sounds promising."

Riordan poured him a full flute. "Enjoy," Riordan said. "Me? I switched to macros one hangover ago."

The captain took the flute. He drained it. He set the empty glass on the oval teak of the table. He rested his hands on the edge and leaned forward. He studied Riordan.

"'Nother flute?" Riordan asked.

"Wouldn't say no."

"Then neither will I."

Riordan filled the flute. The captain swept it up in his hand and lifted it in toast. Riordan raised his beer bottle.

"To us," the captain said.

"Nostrovia," Riordan said.

They clinked glass. The captain sipped then appraised his stemware. "Stuart," he said, nodding with approval. "Shaftesbury."

"You would know," Riordan said.

"So, mind if I sit?"

"Of course not. Misery loves company, especially my company."

"And mine."

"Sí. Tasteless bastard, old Misery."

They both sat in silence, brooding on this. Neither looked at the other.

"Jack," the captain began, "we go back a ways, you and I."

"A ways?"

"Yes."

Riordan mulled this over then shook his head slowly and with no small sadness.

"Only if you call the beheading of my eleven-year-old daughter an 'a ways.'"

That bit of unmentionable yet undeniable horror brought this segment of the conversation to somewhat of an abrupt if temporary halt. Finally, Riordan raised his longneck and sipped then set his bottle down on the teak. He considered the moment: the passage of time: its brevity. And within that brevity, its ceaseless, ceaseless senselessness.

It was as real and palpable as the condensation that descended the bottles and flutes on the table in rivulets, wandering earthward as if lost: the child: missing for seventy-two hours; Riordan and his wife: sleepless and in famine for said hours; the then Detective Inspector Sims Reid treading deliberately up the brick path to their front door in their Northside neighborhood. They can see him out the front window. Middle of the day. Overcast. Autumn. A block from the Burlington Northern yard. The iron clacking of the switching rails, like forged dentures. The grinding hum of the impatient diesels, near diabolical and without cease. DI Sims treading *far* too deliberately. Like a man approaching his own gravestone. Hands searching the empty pockets of his untied raincoat. Perhaps in those pockets the words to tell them. October 1982: We—we found her bicycle.

A senselessness. One that, if you spent your end-of-days wandering and querenting with Plato himself through the olive gardens of the original Akademy, you could not fathom thus. If you hung with Siddhartha Gautama in the vales of Benares as he dispensed his parable of the mustard seed, still you could not fathom thus: Your daughter's beheading. Her rape and murder. Tell us now, oh mage and magi, where is her eternal soul and is she still eleven years and five months and twenty-one days old?

Riordan shut his eyes for a moment. When he opened them he looked across at the captain. Quiet. His eyes averted. Riordan knew he'd killed the messenger as we all do and do all too frequently.

"Sorry," Riordan said.

"Don't be," the captain said.

But in seek of amends, Riordan slid over the copy of *Vancouver Life*. "Here," he said. "I read this."

The captain hesitated then picked up the issue, and Riordan watched the captain's eyes swiftly scan the content.

"Nice little bit," Riordan said. "Up in Vancouver, these poor sods each day drive out to the airport to watch the planes land while they scoff their egg-salad sandwiches."

"I know," the captain said, but Riordan wasn't listening. On he ploughed:

"One of the lunchers, she said she watched the planes land because, get this, she was so scared of flying, she couldn't even *read* Erica Jong."

"Nice punch line."

Riordan didn't even blink, continuing:

"Another simply—and fricking honestly—said he ate lunch there for the same reason he attended NASCAR races."

"In hope for the crashes," the captain finished.

Now Riordan looked up at the captain, but his soused brain still all-too-slowly wheeled.

"Any champers left?" the captain asked.

"Dregs is all."

"Hey, they're Frog dregs. Pour away."

Turned out, there was a half flute left. The captain sipped. Riordan surged on:

"Then the author interviewed this couple. Late middle-aged. Jesus, they came every day to watch in their car-towed

Windstream because his blood brother, Nial, he'd died in the Lockerbie disaster."

"I know," the captain said.

"Not in the plane, but on the ground."

"Sí," the captain said. "The best man at their wedding. Then, later, a falling out and a long grudge of silence."

Riordan had read this, but with his champagne-buzzed brain, the captain's words didn't register, so Riordan waded even deeper: "Died the very day after breaking that silence and buying a plane ticket to visit," he said.

"To be with them," the captain said. "After thirty years."

"Right," Riordan said.

He fell silent, but somehow still the captain's words did not quite register. Riordan took a sip of his Bud. He frowned. Now it registered. He looked up. "Why do you keep doing this?" he asked.

"What?"

"Finishing my sentences. My thoughts."

"Because I know. Knew the guy who wrote it. Polo— Alexander Polo—was a grad student here in the writing program. A year or so after, he sold that piece."

"You knew him?"

"*Of* him. Odd guy. Pretty wife. Two kids. Sons. May be a daughter."

"May be?"

"Jack, I—I just knew of him, as I said."

"Eh, no mind, El Capitan. Save yer breath to cool yer porrige."

He sipped. Then asked:

"So—so what—what happened to him? This Polo?"

"What happens to all of us, I suppose."

"Which is?"

The captain sipped. Appraised the depth of his companion's melancholy.

"Well," he said, taking a stab at levity, "today's evidence has it that we leave our bride at the altar and get drunk watching planes land."

"Fuck you," Riordan said. "I saw a CRJ-200 come blundering in like a gooney and a Beech 1900 land nimble as a hummingbird. I even ID'd Denny Washington's Gulfstream."

"Your old boss."

"Ha! That's rich."

The captain took a moment.

"You know, Jack," he said, "I always had you figured as more of a train guy than a plane guy."

Riordan lifted his beer for a thoughtful moment. "After today," he said, "I'm not even an RV guy." Silence. He then continued, waggling his bottle at the cockpit:

"They—the old couple—they came looking for him, didn't they? For this Polo guy. For him to somehow bestow . . . what'd ya call it? Absolution?"

The captain didn't answer. But Riordan wouldn't concede.

"But by then he'd taken off, right? Right? However," Riordan continued, "undeterred, the two old buggers did the you-know-what anyway. In the pilots' seats. Well?"

"Autopsy—autopsy showed she had onset Lewy body disease."

Riordan paused in mid-sip.

"Good Jesus Christ," he said. "Mad cow disease?"

"Worse."

The two men fell silent. Riordan contemplated his Bud then said:

"The poor dear."

The captain sighed. Then he stood. He grew pensive. Finally he lifted his flute and drained it. "You're gonna sleep here overnight, yes?"

"You going to tow me?"

"Beyond my jurisdiction."

"That's less than encouraging. The county Mounties then?"

The captain ran his fingers through his own thick, dark hair and laughed. "I'll call Deputy Dawg," he said. He stepped away from the table and stood at the stair leading down to the front exit.

"Who?"

"The deputy sheriff. Name's Doug, poor bastard."

"Ah, as in Huckleberry Hound," said Riordan, regaining some minor semblance of the upper hand. "No shortage of wit amongst *our* officers of the peace."

The ringtone of his cell phone awakened him the next morning—September the 11th. As yesterday, it was his son, John. And as yesterday, though not this time in his coffin, Riordan had just as much trouble extricating his phone from his trousers pocket. He wasn't *in* the bed but sprawled *on* it, and he still wore his full Big Sur wedding getup: what had Bea called him? The marquis of Abingdon? Avingdon? When he brought the phone to his ear, the displeasure and ache in every fiber of his being told him he had inflicted upon himself a hangover of legendary proportions: one his father would have described as five pounds of shit stuffed into a one-pound sack. He pressed the green answer key, and seeking to lessen the damage of his son's voice in his throbbing head he held the phone at a distance from his actual ear.

"Dad? You there? Dad!?"

"Sí," he groaned.

"Dad! Is that you? Dad?"

He groaned again and by twisting at the waist and stiff-arming the mattress like an all-conference tailback, he somehow managed to sit up, though the exertion induced an iron-lung gasp.

"Yes, it's me, Son. What—what is it? And the Christ's the time?" He rubbed his eyes with the back of his free wrist. Out the windows: pale, barely light skies. Morning? Early morning? Early evening?

"Dad, listen to me. You listening?"

"Yes, Son. What?"

"Dad: Turn *on* the TV."

He thought for a moment.

"Did you hear me, Dad? Turn. On. The TV."

"Christ, Son, I—I don't know if I even *have* TV."

"Dad, I gotta go. TURN. ON. THE TV!"

"What channel?"

"Any. It doesn't matter. It doesn't fucking matter."

. . . .

Riordan saw his first jet contrail carve its half-comforting, half-sinister scar in the empty blue sky a few days after. Doubtless a military plane: an F-15 perhaps or a Navy Tomcat. Bea was at a subdued campaign strategy meeting and an even more subdued fund-raiser, so Riordan had piloted the motor coach back to the airport, idling for a brief time at the end of the runway. An hour earlier in a half-sheepish reminder of his wedding-day petulance, he had stacked the British Columbia license plates—PNM 103—atop the magazine and aerograms and poems and set them on the passenger seat. He vowed to keep them as penitence after he sold this ten-wheeled and six-figure albatross.

He gripped the wheel. Through the massive curvature of the front windshield and beyond the airport's wire fencing, the runway stretched seemingly to the far-distant mountains, the runway's heat islands shimmering like dark lagoons in a darker river. The tallest mountain, Lolo Peak, stood still as steel and as blue. Snow-capped and despite all come to pass, yet grasping the sky. On the tarmac a few small motionless single-engine planes were still scattered here and there, each exuding a sense of having been hastily abandoned. Or more eerily of having been placed there like clapboard replicas, perhaps to dupe the world into thinking nothing had changed.

Alas, nothing had.

II

CASTLEGAR

1941

(Prelude)

*I*f you were Phillip or Roger or Nial, you could readily strong-arm the Ariel's handlebars, twisting them as easily as wringing out a wet tea towel, so that motorbike and sidecar now stood by the curb of the tiny cottage like an annealed and iron chariot. But Phillip had been pronounced by the War Office as missing and presumed dead, his Sunderland flying boat shot down by the Luftwaffe over the channel the year before. And Nial? He stood on alert in Abingdon, ninety or so miles to the southwest, await with the rest of RAF 63 Squadron's crew of Avro twin-engine Manchester bombers. So with the other two either deceased or disposed of, that left Roger and now this same Roger dismounted from the Ariel and after a moment he peeled off his leather headgear and shook out his thick blond hair. Ever wary and ever the warrior, he took a deep breath and sought his bearings. Latitude and longitude: 52.31 North, 0.17 East. Time: 15:11 hours. Good Christ. Now the task ahead rung bells *in his head and his heart. Well, a volunteer's worth ten pressed men, his father used to say, and though Roger had indeed volunteered for this unholy mission, he felt in his soul like the press gang's last conscript: you know, the poor git split seconds before licensing hours end and you're otherwise scot-free and safely home to bed.*

He looked about. So this was Godmanchester—an odd name and when you parsed it both fitting and ill-figured. The cottage itself looked to be a story and a half with a gabled roof and shuttered windows. A rickety wood fence staggered out from the sides of the cottage, encircling its back garden erratically as though it was of its own all-thumbs construction. Now in the air came the pounding noise of a hammer against an anvil, a clanging and ringing and echoing, and came then a bellowing—a deep male bellowing—and a shrieking and then a euphoric clapping of four or more hands and then the giddy laughter of a young and happy woman or, perhaps, that of a beautiful and gleeful young girl.

One

(London: A few days earlier)

This far into Hell you had to actually *listen*—i.e., pay attention—to hear the daemonics: the whistling of the bombs as they swooped down to obliterate their targets and the explosions as the bombs accomplished their assigned tasks and the horrible *ningggggg-ningggg-ninggggg* drone of the Luftwaffe war machines far above but raining down without surcease—deafening as a plague of industrial-spawned wasps—not to mention the incessant and blunt *thupp-thupp*-thumping of the anti-aircraft guns—like siege cannon (which for all purposes they were)—all this after all these months you would have to pay attention to if you wanted to hear. (And who'd've wanted to?)

Mac, however—Charles William George McEwan—possessed a cerebral cortex that had since banished this audible horror to "muted" if not "mute." After his day job as superintendent of London Transport (buses), he toiled as chief air raid warden for Kenton District Seven—"toiled" not quite the word, for Mac bore his duties and responsibilities with the seriousness and gravity—and this is no exaggeration—as Athenian General Themistocles must have at the gates of Thermopylae.

Mac especially loved his steel hat (though in reality it was forged from tin) with its leather chin strap and its white "W" for "warden" standing strict at attention in the front above its brim. Loved his wide cotton armband that he boasted on his right upper arm: *ARW—Chief.* Mac too loved his dead son Phillip whose Sunderland flying boat had not only been shot down over the channel by the Luftwaffe but subsequently against all Geneva Conventions of war had been strafed and sunk. All aboard drowned or declared MIA. (Mac possessed not a whit of factual evidence of this latter abomination save for the certitude of his own anger and crippling grief.) Letters of condolence from the War Office and even the king. The latter personally signed, *George VI, R&I* (Rex and Imperator). Loved too his beautiful young daughter, Susan, with a burning-bush bushel of black hair, nearing fourteen and an evacuee up in Godmanchester and lodged with his wife's uncle's cousin (or some such) Ben the blacksmith. He recited these things that he so coveted and loved on his nightly patrols, recited them over and over and over here in war-grim England like an egg-and-chips mantra, a mantra of possible (though dubious) liberation.

ON THIS DARK NIGHT IN January of 1941 as the horror-show bursts of blinding light and deafening sound thrust themselves up into the sky above the City—before they whitewashed themselves across the stars and the clouds—Mac patrolled as he always did. West along Streatfield and right up Kenton Lane before retracing his steps south down Kenton then back east along Streatfield (their house was 133) before again turning north to circle around the outer crescent—that would be Portland—then pace off the inner crescent (Langland)—in essence tightening with his footsteps a noose. And though he doubtless knew his way he was a lost man, our Mac—you feel the loss of a child (no matter its age at its demise) as an amputee loses his appendage yet still vividly experiences its presence: viscerally and deeply and with blind desperation, seeking to regain at least a single momentary access to its use, a tortuous desperation that lasts forever.

This night, beneath his black and belted pea jacket, Mac wore a submarine commander's wool mock turtle—scratchy as a Brillo—but a welcome shield against the damp sop of night air that otherwise rheumed through his aging bones and congealed his marrow. As he circled this inner crescent (Langland), he knew he would have to confront the señora, Marte Benité, who lived at 146 and would be reading her poetry books under a blanketed hood of candlelight. As she did every night.

"Señora."

"Señor Mac. Sí?"

In his mind, Mac always employed the word "substantial" to describe both her physical bearing and that of her inner presence. He invariably summoned forth the image of Madame Defarge in Dickens (that he'd never read) or that of Pilar, the de facto guerrilla leader in Hemingway's newest book (that Mac also hadn't read but he'd bought and sent in the post for Christmas to his daughter up in Godmanchester).

"Lights out, oy?" Mac suggested to the señora.

"I wait for you, Señor Mac."

"As the Luftwaffe waits for you, sí?"

"Yes, Señor Mac."

Mac turned to go.

"How is your daughters, Señor Mac?"

"Daughter. And she's safe."

"Buenos."

Mac turned away to resume his rounds. The señora waggled the book from under her cowl.

"*Blood Wedding*, Señor Mac."

"Aren't they all?"

"This time, Señor Mac, we *will* defeat the Fascistas."

And together they might have except that Mac turned away not quite as crisply as he always did, and the bootheel of his Wellington clipped Señora Benité's garden grass beneath which lurked a Luftmine-A magnetic parachute mine. This disruption of the magnetic device contained inside caused the (34) P fuse to detonate, and with an explosive outgush of razor-sharp shrapnel, the landmine blew Mac's legs off just above the knees as cleanly and instantly as if they had been severed and dispatched by the glinting scimitar of a khan.

Lore has it that land mines were first deployed in China in the thirteenth century by Qianxia Li as the Song Dynasty fought to stave off the invading Mongols. Supposedly Pedro Navarro designed a working land mine in the early 1500s and this design was thus perfected by Samuel Zimmerman of Germany in 1600. Three hundred and forty-one years later, in the early years of the Second World War, a Luftwaffe Heinkel He III spat out its cache of Luftmine parachute mines over Kenton, London, and one drifted gently down to nestle in the garden at 146 Langland, lying in wait for the soft yet not insignificant detonation of Mac's Wellington bootheel.

It was inconceivable to Mac as he floundered there on his back buried in the damp and razored ground that he might survive. What were the odds here in the chill and crushing darkness? To Mac, not a chance in ten thousand. Though not a prayerful man, he yet forged his peace with whatever force or power had genesised into existence the universe and the planets, not to mention the wry and gelid force that had spawned this patch of muck and tears known as England. Mac forged his peace with his unhappy and pious wife, forged it with his beautiful daughter who was "apprenticed" to a blacksmith (though his lips managed not a smile, his heart did); forged too his peace with Phillip, now fallen, and in the instant just before he blacked out (and this the most important of all), he finally found his peace with the German fliers: the ones who had circled back upon Phillip's downed Sunderland flying boat as it listed and filled with the bracken waters of the channel, those same German fliers who with their MG-131 and MG-81Z ma-chine guns had summarily executed all the Sunderland's sur-viving crew and had stolen from Mac for all eternity his only and begotten son.

Two

Roger was damned if he could fathom a gate in the crippled fence that surrounded the cottage. He circled the entire thing and then back again but no gate. Made no sense. None. He thought to call out but the clanging of hammer on iron from the smithy shed rendered that moot. And he didn't want to risk an attempt at summiting the splinted and rickety thing. Not in his uniform. The quartermaster would pay him bloody what for if he ripped or tarnished his trousers, save alone his jacket. No. Surely there must exist an alternative. By the time he'd again fully circumnavigated the property and stood not yards from the cottage's planked front door, a dog inside began to yip furiously. Some sort of Pekinese he guessed. He'd grown up on his father's farm in Dumfries and Galloway with English sheep dogs and blue heelers, and while he loved and revered all dogs, small yappy dogs still tested his virtue. Then the front door opened.

A middle-aged woman stood in its opening. Not heavy-set but not inconsequential. Light gray hair tauted back from her face. She took Roger's measure with her eyes in less than a tick save alone its tock. The dog, indeed a Pekinese, continued to yip at her feet.

"Is this official like?" she asked.

"Well, in a way. I've come to fetch Susan."

Still the yipping. The woman ankled the dog away and back, but it took no respite. "For God's sake, Milly," she said to it, "cease your whinging."

"I'm about—ah—Mr. McEwan."

"Mac?"

"Yes. I've a letter. In ink."

"I would hope so. Millicent!" she snapped at the dog. "And—and you are?"

"Group Captain Grey, RAF."

"Yes," she said, somehow pleased with this. "Yes indeed you are."

ONCE THROUGH THE KITCHEN AND into the back garden, Roger wound his way along the irregular path which had stones moguled into the soft ground and which led to the smithy's work shed. It was more of a lean-to than even the crudest of sheds and in its sole grace it boasted a stovepipe chimney. The main sidewall was a single massive sheet of corrugated iron that was propped against and affixed to the top of a relic stone edifice that might've been assembled stone by stone by Druids. The front of the shed was thus a broad triangle of that same corrugation gapped by a heavily planked door—more like a crude gate—which had swung to the half-open.

"Susan?" he tried to call. "Mr. Morris?" but his callings were extinguished by (this close) the deafening *Klang-Klang-kuh-KLANG!* from the shed. God, was she really apprenticed to this brute or had it been one of Phillip's (bless his soul) leg-pulls? On either side of the door, stacked against the outer wall, were the massive iron bracelets that were the tires of wagon wheels and the *Klang-Kuh-Klang-Kuh-KLANG!* afforded no surcease and in a single step Roger grasped and scraped open the heavy door and beheld her. There: behind the wide pan of the forge, beside Ben, his thick shoulders hunched like a Minotaur's beneath his sweat-grimed shirt. Above the forge, a hood and flue of blackened and dented metal hung as if no longer bound to time or space and beneath this incongruity the red-hot coals in the forge's pan glowed with a Mephistophelian light. Ben held a ball-peen hammer unstruck in mid-stroke and Susan beside him—her face a brighter rose than the very coals in the forge's pan—Susan held a long string of black iron, narrow as a knitting needle. With her beautiful flushed face and her curled dark hair tendrilled atop her shoulders she looked to Roger like a gypsy princess, her eyes dark and shining and immediate when she saw him.

"Captain Grey?" she said in half disbelief. "Captain Grey?"

"Please, Roger," he said.

She swallowed and glanced at Ben then fixed her eyes back on him. "Captain Grey," she repeated. "Is—is it Mum?" she asked.

He shook his head, unable to say.

"It's Dad, right?" her voice breaking. "Dad?"

Roger took a moment.

"I—I've got the sidecar," he said.

1959

Roger put the Cub down hard in the stiff crosswind, its ancient wings and fuselage flapping like a Chinese kite. "D'ye take Susan up in this tattered shite of a thing?" Nial hollered forward, his brogue as rich and smooth as the scent from a briar pipe.

"Ha," Roger responded backwards over his shoulder. "Susan hasn't so much as been in a kiddie swing since Phillip and her dad."

The tiny plane skewed and slowed on the runway, the grind of the engine quieting, and Roger waggled the rudder to guide the plane towards a cluster of other single-engines off to the left.

"Khrushchev's landing at Idlewild in a few hours," Nial observed.

"Let's hope his Tupolev lands as gracefully as this little sweetheart," Roger said. He cut the engine as the Cub rolled to its berth. "Those Russki jets are all left feet."

"And I've cold ones," Nial said. The craft stilled and Nial thought for a moment then body-checked open the rear hatch and two-feet-first bailed the single meter earthward. The shadow of the wing diagonal'd on the brown grass of the aerodrome like the shadow of a guillotine blade.

"Why won't you believe it was Susan's idea?" Roger asked him. They were in the beverage room of the Trail, BC, Legion Hall by the Columbia River. Plaster walls. Square Formica tables. The wandering waiter had a round-rimmed metal tray the size of a Greyhound bus's steering wheel and he bore it and its sparse population of eight-ounce draft glasses atop his right palm, and inserting his thumb and first three fingers of his left hand inside their contents he plucked four of the slender glasses from the tray and set them between the two friends as deftly as a manicurist. Roger had placed a dollar bill with the queen's young profile under the ashtray and without a word the waiter snared the bill and fished from his waist-apron two quarters and a dime and shoveled them onto the table.

"Keep a quarter," Roger told him.

"That'll be a first, Rog," the waiter said.

"Mind yer manners, Tim," Roger said. "This is me best mate from over the sod."

The waiter pocketed the quarter.

"Then let's hope he visits more often."

Barely afternoon. A weekday. The beverage room pretty much deserted and dank. The walls sweating and barren. An odious and odorous kinship of smoke, urine, and beer.

"Cheers," Roger said lifting one of the tulip-lipped glasses. He swallowed a goodly portion of the brew, his Adam's apple bobbing with each drachm. "Ah," he said, setting the near polished-off glass on the tabletop. "Gectar of the nods." He studied his friend. Nial lifted his own draft glass and in a single swallow drained it. He set the empty on the table and lifted the second.

"Cheers," he said to Roger.

"Salud," Roger said, lifting his own second.

Nial fell silent.

"Rog," he said after a moment. "What if it isn't you? Not your fault?"

"Let's have another round," Roger suggested.

"I mean, not your little swimmers to blame."

Roger didn't answer, busily scanning the empty room. "Where's that bloody Tim gone?" he complained. "And with me flamin' bloody quarter?"

"SHE'S TAKEN TO POEMS," ROGER told Nial. Now the two friends—a two-man band of brothers—were walking along the banks of the Columbia. The great river here in the Canadian Rockies but a sapling but still swelling with promise. A parkside path between the grasses. Trees yet to color. A distant surround of mountains like a towering granite theatre. All this and a late-September sky unscarred by cloud.

"What—what about one of those fertility places?" Nial suggested. "They've even one in Edinburg."

Roger didn't answer, mired in thought. After a few steps farther along, he slowed and said:

"Studies them, she does. The poems. Not in a classroom but via the post. From some ponce in Spain or Mexico or some other bloody place. Ordered the books and everything. More'n a few quid, but—"

"Ye didn't answer me," Nial said. "About the fertility places."

Nor did Roger answer yet. Instead, he said:

"I have to fly to Castlegar. Then Prince George. Tonight."

"You bully her," Nial said.

"A little. I'll leave you the DeSoto. You can take her to dinner."

Nial sighed.

"This is Susan," he said. "Susan."

Roger stopped, as did Nial. Both men at six feet tall, they could look directly into each other's eyes, though the lankier Roger seemed the taller. Roger's hair thick and blond and Brylcreem'd. Nial's dark as a matinee idol's.

"What this is," Roger told Nial, "is strictly clinical. She may swot bollocking poetry, but she's an RN in her core."

It was warm, and both were in shirtsleeves. White, as per the decade. Cotton undershirts vee'd beneath their unbuttoned collars. Then either on impulse or intent Roger held out his bare arms and displayed the undersides of his wrists. The jag of a scar on the left one. Healed but never annealed. By design. Ancient. Conceived and first implemented by antediluvian warriors.

"Show me yours," he said to Nial.

Nial on reflex already had his hands hidden in his trouser pockets.

"Show me," Roger repeated.

But Nial kept his scar buried.

"Rog," he said, "I canna do it. She's Susan."

"No she's not. She's an RN. And me? Me?"

Nial offered no response. They both stood silent. They could hear the Columbia gathering momentum.

"Me?" Roger said softly. "Fuck, mate, I'm Roger. Group Captain fucking Roger. I took her from what family she had left, and now, because of *me*, she can't have one of her own."

Silence. Both sought diversion, so they looked about. The soaring mountains. The immaculate sky. Even the breeze whispering time's secrets to the leaves of the trees. All this incalculable grandeur diminishing the two aviators to the infinitesimal.

Roger faced him.

"And with you," he said to Nial. "Well, the little sprog'd have me blood, wouldn't he? Enough to mean something." He paused. He looked as square into Nial's eyes as brothers on the Ark. "Mean everything, when ye think of it."

Nial hesitated. On the brink but knowing full well the heart as the slipperiest of slopes. So he pronounced:

"No, Rog, I—"

But Roger cut him short:

"Reconsider. At least. And dinner. And not the bloody Legion."

"Aye," Nial said. "Dinner. But I won't be changin' me mind."

"Me blood," Roger said, his eyes and voice cast down. "He'd have me blood."

T he menu boasted T-bones and lamb chops and breaded sole. They drank gimlets, and the waiters and busboys who serviced the other tables kept glancing at her. At once slender and succulent. A not-of-this-place elegance. She wore her hair up and wore elbow-length white gloves to accessorize a bodiced crinoline dress, one with a décolleté neckline. A string of pearls on her neck and cleavage that even the other women in the room would have defended as natural and sea-watered. They were instead the famed Scottish freshwater pearls from the River Tay. A wedding gift from Roger's frail grandmother, a priceless string her husband had half filched from the legendary jeweler Cairncross of Perth the same day the Titanic had sailed.

Now those pearls lay like grace itself around this beauty's slender neck. She lowered her eyes to inspect the menu and the string of pearls fluttered above her modest cleavage like tiny swans. And though this the grandest most posh hotel in Trail, its dining room's menu graced no wine list save that laminated to its last page:

Black Tower $7 per bottle
Kelowna Red $4 per bottle
Blue Nun $8 per bottle

"I've had the Mother Superior," Nial announced in a whisper. He grinned.

"Don't be blasphemous," Susan scolded. "Besides, I've heard you're supposed to drink red with steak."

"I was considering the lamb."

"Red with that too. At least so I've heard."

Nial took a moment, watching her. She lowered her eyes.

"Say that again?" he asked.

"What? About the lamb?"

"That that's what you've heard."

"Whatever for?"

"Your accent," Nial said. "I was of a mind earlier that Roger's lost his."

"Not so much as lost as dispatched, I should think."

Nial sipped his gimlet. He ached to change the subject.

"How—how do you find being a nurse?" he asked.

"Turn left at the hospital?" she suggested.

For some reason the glibness of her quip stung him, stung him deeply, and he couldn't find the words.

"Sorry," she said. She reached a hand across the table but only halfway before she withdrew it back into her lap. She lowered her eyes. "That wasn't fair," she said.

He sipped, pensive. "Nothing's fair," he said. "Nothing."

He sought to change the subject.

"Roger," he said, in search of amends, "Roger told me yer studying poetry."

"By correspondence," she said. "By the post."

"A Spanish bloke? Yer headmaster?"

"Roger seems to think so. Though the lessons arrive from The Dalles."

"The Dales?"

"In Oregon. The States. With two *l*'s."

"Aye. Most Spanish sounding, that: The Dalles. Wait, Las Dalles, sí?"

She laughed.

"They're—they're sonnets," she said.

At this he fell quiet. Sonnets? He looked at her. For wasn't she the most radiant creature the gods had ever granted him bane or blight to behold: the dark eyes, the carriage, the pearls, and the clumsy and self-mocking white gloves. Beatific. He didn't know a limerick from a laundry list but surely—surely—that face'd be worthy of a thousand sonnets penned by a thousand what?—sonneteers? Sí. At least by this one. And so deciding, he announced quietly, "It must be pitch black, the bedroom, pitch black. And absolutely no touching. And, most of all, I must be drunk. Pissed drunk."

She said nothing. Acquiescent? Who could tell. Not even she.

The waiter arrived at their table. A short man, his employers had furthered his burden by cladding him in black tuxedo pants and the clipped crimson jacket of a toreador. He bore his pen and order pad as though about to issue a parking violation.

"Have yis made up yer minds?" he asked.

"Actually," Nial said, "the lass here would have a drop of the grape. As would thee senn."

"Eh, then I'll be a mome," the waiter said. "It's not nightly we get folks ordering other than the hard stuff."

They laughed when the waiter left. He looked at her. So lovely. A universe away.

"So black it is blue?" he said.

"The wine?"

"The bedroom."

This stopped her.

"Utterly dark," he clarified.

"So—so you won't know I'm cross-eyed?"

"So I won't know you're not."

THE DESOTO HAD A PUSHBUTTON transmission mounted on the dash to the left of the steering wheel—quite impressive to a postwar Brit like Nial—but he thought the car itself when it cornered was as unwieldy as a catamaran. And Trail, British Columbia, in 1959 was a city of corner after corner: even the hairpin turns had hairpin turns.

"Ray Sonin," Susan said.

Nial didn't respond. Instead, he intensified his focus on the task at hand: not getting them killed. He gripped the steering wheel, heaving at it as if trying to reforge it into an airplane rudder and leaned forward. Frowning and peering into the darkness. In search of sobriety.

"Take the next right," Susan said.

You follow your headlights and you always get home, they said in those days, and somehow Nial did. At her driveway he nudged the DeSoto up the mild grade until it bussed the lip of the closed garage door and turned off the engine. He was sweating. Drained. He'd flown forty-six night missions over Frankfurt and Dresden and Kraków, the anti-aircraft fire in the darkness shrouding you like exploding garments, but this mission tonight—this one had his soul somehow strained and thinned, a veneer where used to exist what he thought was an oak. He took a deep breath. That was better. Thought back to their drive home.

"Ray—Ray who?" he asked Susan.

"Ray Sonin," Susan said.

"Who is?"

"This English duff on a Toronto radio station. CFRB, I think. Does a Brit radio show every Saturday afternoon. 'Calling All Britons.'"

"Wait, you get Toronto radio stations way out here?"

"No. But Roger found a way to get them via short wave."

"But they're—they're amplitude modified."

"I know. But he somehow manages."

Here in the high Rockies at this juncture of the late 1950s the sky was dark, dark and as glittering as a tiara of ice and eternity. And absolutely, utterly still. The earth in caesura: clutching its breath.

"Roger—Roger says that one day, computers will be as small as tellys and that we'll all own one and talk to each other on them."

"Roger thinks we should be in Sputniks with the chimps."

She offered neither reply nor contradiction. A moment passed.

"Do—do you like my pearls?" she asked.

There in the driver's seat of his blood brother's DeSoto he turned his head, and in that primeval darkness he beheld his blood brother's wife: radiant and lithe, her black eyes moist and tearless.

"We mustn't touch," he decreed again. "Or kiss. And utter bloody dark."

CONSIDER FOR AN INSTANT THE sheer range of love and lust. The fetid couplings of Neanderthals in rut. The luted serenades of fops and fools beneath an inamorata's balcony. Our two lovers hovered amidst this trope like string puppets, each the other's puppeteer and each the gladder for it: See? How can you not touch? Not kiss?

"Tell me something."

"What?"

"Anything."

"Your skin tastes like—"

"Like what?"

"Like morning."

Like morning indeed. Ah, but the tens of thousands of ensuing mornings—three decades of them less a year—contained not a word exchanged between this twosome band of brothers, though Roger, for his part, did compose and pen the following on one of those same sky-blue, diaphanous aerograms as the last letter home from Phillip that Susan read on the train to Godmanchester and till end of days cherished. As for this?

21 January 1960

Nial. I've good news and bad news. But first, you simmering bastard. No wonder you cleared the fuck off so soon before the morning I got back. It was supposed to be clinical, right? She being a nurse and all, right? As we agreed, right? You were to implant her not bloody enchant her. Seed her not bloody steal her.

But ye did. So get the fuck ta shite, ye miserable cunt. I thought our bond thicker than mere blood. Our brotherhood more sacred than same-last-name fucked-about siblings. Obviously, I was dead stropping wrong.

Now, me fuck, the bad news: she's not pregnant.

Next, the good news: she's not pregnant. Which means I won't be reminded of your bloody betrayal every day for the rest of me fucking life.

The rest of me fucking life.

Our marriage may never recover, but don't you dare get any ideas, you bloody bastard. You'll never have her. I'll kill her first; kill us both.

All three!

Fuck.

Fuckety-fuckety-fuck!

Ridiculous.

Nial, Nial, Nial. Fuck, mate. I dinna know whether ta shit or wind me watch, and now, you sodden bastard, ye got me writing in Scots. When, if ever, will anything change? When you read this letter? Pisser is, yi'll never read this letter. Ever. Me beloved mate. Me dearest poxy-est beloved mate.

~~Rog~~ Roger

True to his word, Roger never sent it. He sealed it, licked and thumbed a Royal Mail Canada stamp upon the tissue of its upper right-hand shoulder, but he never mailed it. And thus its truths and confessions and absolutions lingered, sadly, for years in that withering emotional corridor of reticence and silence which sooner or later we all traverse.

1988

A few weeks before Nial died, ITV screened the film adaptation of John Hersey's *The War Lover*, set in Britain during WWII and starring Steve McQueen and Robert Wagner as bomber pilots. Nial changed the channel as he had sworn a long-standing aversion to any books or films about the war—especially ones involving saturate bombing runs over cities. But over the subsequent passage of days, Nial grudgingly and gradually capitulated, admitting that the real reason he had chosen to not watch that particular war movie was not the bombing runs nor the war, but rather the love story: the love triangle between McQueen's and Wagner's characters and the luminously beautiful Daphne played by Shirley Anne Field. And so one morning in early December, after he had berated himself enough for his cowardice and petty adamance, he caved and wandered down through the December rains to the cramped video section of his local off-license to see if they had it.

"Nada," Beg the manager told him. "Ye want a classic? We've *Flashdance*."

"*Flashdance*? Jennifer what's-'er-name?"

"Beals."

"I'm not here for Jennifer bloody Beals. I want McQueen and Robert Wagner and that Daphne bird."

"Nial, d'ye think we've fuckin' shelf space for such shite? It's in bloody black and white."

"So?"

"So? So?"

"Where'm I te get it, then?"

"Do ye not have a library card?"

"What's a library?"

"Get te fuck, Nial. I'm running a serious enterprise here—a prospering enterprise, I might fuckin' add, with no thanks te the likes of fuckin' ye."

But the Lockerbie Library was also a toss.

"We can order it," the librarian told him.

"Order?"

"Buke-speak. From the Dumfries branch. Won't cost."

"Well, eh—" He weighed his options.

> *Your skin tastes like—*
> *Like what?*

"Be here Friday," she added, a fleshy, gray-haired temptress with dangling bifocals accentuating her bosom. "Make a great supper-and-the-pictures," she teased, nibbling her lower lip.

"Ta, but, er, I was long ago spoken for, ye see."

IT WAS ASYMMETRICAL, NIAL DECREED, the bloody movie—at least the love triangle. The barracks and bedroom scenes too sanitized—especially the barracks scenes. But why bloody quibble? As for the combat and bombing scenes? Sanitized? Christ, they could've been cathetered by the filmmakers like a blood-draw of terror from his own bowels. The claustrophobic cockpit—five men lashed Gosport-to-Gosport[8] in a steel-and-rivet straightjacket. And the noise: the harrowing roar of the engines as the B-17s screamed and cartwheeled like pockmarked rollercoasters, hounded and bitten by packs of enemy fighters through the demented clouds. Not the least the strafes of machine-gun fire, gatling the entirety of the sky and the fliers' minds with shrieking wheems of insidious and ravenous shrapnel. Almost exhausting, Nial thought. No, te shite with the "almost."

Exhausting. Bloody exhausting.

AS WERE THE LOVE SCENES. The *romance* scenes, more to the point. Sanitized or not. As, after all these years, were his own:

8. An RAF term for the snouty voice-pipe masks aviators wore to communicate with each other and their squadron mates.

The spill of her hair: untangling across the pillowcase in the bed-room's blindness, untangling like a blackcurrant bush afire, a throw of sparks splintering the darkness, shocking.

•

Utterly dark.
So—so you won't know I'm cross-eyed?
So I won't know you're not.

DAYS TO COME, NIAL THOUGHT and planned and busied himself. He watched the film yet again. Then he decided:

19 December 1988
Lockerbie, Scotland

Dear Roger.

I so, so ache to finally refer to you again as Rog and to Susan as Suze after these near-thirty years. Is that even mildly agreeable? Plus, I want to call both of you by those lovely diminutives to your faces and so, surprise!, to that end I've bought a ticket to YVR[9] for this January the 21st. I'm to drive down to Heath-row the day before and stay at the London hotel by

9. The IATA airport code for Vancouver International Airport in Vancou-ver, BC.

Marble Arch (can't remember the hotel's name but it's far, far too posh and going to cost me a packet) and then get up in the morg and soapbox in the park for an hour (against The Iron Lady's rape of our pensions, maybe?), then rattle on the Tube out to Heathrow and board the flight. It's an L-1011 as opposed to a DC-("Death Cart")10, so I just might make it over the pond.

I don't know what else to write in this. I'd say our three hearts were broken those three decades ago but hearts don't really break; they just slowly bow and cave beneath time's burden, and these days mine's quite bowed, and more than mildly caved. I broke my promise to myself a few weeks past and rented The War Lover. *Steve McQueen. A young Bob Wagner. And a radiant Daphne. And now? These years later? Well, Steve McQueen's snuffed it. Bob Wagner's snuffed his wiff. And Daphne? Never heard of again.*

Made me think. And feel like shite. And think. And feel like shite. And buy a plane ticket. And write this.

And feel like absolute fucking shite.

Got your Vancouver address from, Roger, your sister, Pam. Has lived a few streets away all these years. We

never spoke. Was surprised and tickled when I asked.
And don't feel the need to meet me at YVR. I can
find me own way. If you're not home, I'll completely
understand.

Ta,
Nial.

THE NEXT MORNING, DECEMBER THE 20th, 1988, Nial
walked the letter and its envelope down to the Lockerbie post
office—he was cheesed as to what the postage cost. "For this
wee shite of a thing?" he complained to the clerk.

"For fuck's sake, Nial, ye clerked here thee sen for twenty
year."

"Ye've no need to bloody remind me."

"It's destined for t'other end of world," the clerk pointed out.
"What d'ye expect?"

"Just that it gets read," he admitted.

COME THE EARLY EVENING, HE dropped the movie off at
the library (tucking it through the outside return slot) and then
popped into the off-license and bought a bottle of Black Tower
and one of Blue Nun. The scornful shite Beg in absentia. He
paid and as he stepped back out into the narrow street, the shop
bell tingled and, an ex-postman but an RAF lifer, he looked up.
The clouded sky lifeless, deserted. Save that far above him—
5.87 miles above him to be exact—that day's Pan Am flight 103
buffeted invisibly overhead in the stratosphere, all-of-a-piece

and landing safely several uneventful hours later at Kennedy Airport in New York, this day's incarnation of Flight 103 a day away from being ordained by whomever's colonels or prophets or gods to fall from the sky.

Three

The cockpit voice recorder of the *Clipper Maid of the Seas*'s (Pan Am 103's) next-day flight revealed upon playback a "loud noise"—a slightly muffled explosion followed by a 180-millisecond hissing noise as the detonation crippled the plane's communications system. While the passengers in the aircraft didn't hear the hissing sound, they surely heard the explosion. One of them, a young German girl of eleven years seated in 32B and traveling with her mother asked, "Was war das, Mutter?"[10] to which her prescient mother in 32A responded only by seizing her daughter's hand and drawing her close to her as if wishing somehow to return the child to the imagined safety of her womb.

10. What was that, Mother?

Nial also heard the explosion, though to his war-tuned ear it seemed crisper, more dire. This was a minute or two after 7:00 p.m. He was standing in his kitchen preparing a late supper, a western omelet with green onions and bell peppers, Westphalian ham and chèvre. The kitchen window's curtains were drawn open. He'd cracked and whisked three brown eggs in a Portmeirion china bowl and had just now poured those eggs into the buttery skillet. On the burner (gas), the eggs began to sizzle and under his spatula began to shirr, but he heard in the sky above that crisp *bhoomk!* and he knew. All those night-bombing runs forty-plus years earlier. Our warriors wear their battle time for all eternity, like skins on their souls, and this night both Nial's own skin and his soul's knew. He instinctively turned off the skillet and looked out and up through the kitchen window. In the night's sky, through the shifting clouds: an orange glow, like a meteor, but to his trained eye nowhere near as benign.

•

HE LIVED OUT NEAR TUNDERGARTH Church on the outskirts of Lockerbie, lived in a one-bedroom fifteenth-century cottage with an upgraded-to-tile roof and an upgraded-to-gas fireplace. This night he dismissed his brain's reproach of fetching a cardigan or shedding his slippers, but he did not dismiss snatching up his military-grade hand-held halogen searchlight which he kept by the front door. Thus equipped he opened the door and stepped outside. He could see in the near distance the darkened silhouette of the church and its steeple. Ancient. The roofed lych-gate opening onto the graveyard. The haunted upright gravestones in the cemetery like the disquieting mouths of the choir invisible. Though in reality, all of it but stone and mortar and blood, each and all impervious to mere men and their frantic and frenzied prayer. As so Nial thought. But then he witnessed something even he would never have conceived possible: the massive nose cone of a 747 jetliner—perfectly intact and cleanly sheared from its rearward fuselage—rocketed down from the night sky like some sort of rogue reentry vehicle and drove itself nose first into the church's damp winter earth. But if that were not enough, then in the distant sky an eruption of apocalyptic light cast up into the darkness and then the thunderous sounds of explosions from Lockerbie proper as the fuselage, wings, and great engines of that 747 hammered down upon the houses, shops, and people, delivering a swath of destruction and death to the town of his birth.

•

BUT THE NOSE CONE: IT lay in the earth and the darkness like the snouted head and neck of some enormous metallic beast, on its left side and, despite the impact, still mostly intact. When Nial shone the searchlight's beam upon it, each illuminated portion seemed to shimmer like a light under water. Indeed a misty rain began to fall. At the entrance to the wreckage he found it crisscrossed and barred by its internal viscera of wire and conduit and by shredded steel, as if some bungled postmortem had already been performed. On the ground about his feet, the spillage of contents of the overhead compartments—duty-free liquor and oversize perfume bottles everywhere and rope-handled designer carrier bags rolfing out their troves of brightly colored garments and footwear. He shone the light deeper into the interior seeking survivors, and his Royal Air Force self commanded *Enter! Rescue them!* while his Royal Mail self cautioned *Crime scene; terrorist attack.* In the distance the town continued to erupt in volcanic flames, and then the dark sky became a great towering sheet of fire all the way up to the clouds as the two hundred–plus tons of jet fuel—already ablaze—rained down. Watching such horror, he instinctively chose compromise: thus did he run the torch beam upward and across the plane's portholes—nine or ten of them and then the windshield of the cockpit. He had to somehow clamber up there and look through them. A 747 on its side is taller than a two-story building, but it had flattened somewhat with the horrific force of the impact. So with the halogen torch prised between his chin and his collarbone he somehow found enough foothold and handhold that after several minutes and badly bloodied hands he stood atop it. Now came the quest for survivors. But when he shone the light through those portholes he saw and witnessed something out of a bizarre carnival funhouse: the first-class passengers still strapped in their seats and lolling downward over their arm rests with the limpness of fresh corpses. Steadfastly he shuffled his way towards the cockpit, porthole by porthole. Now did he curse the foolish haste of his footgear, his bloody stupid slippers. But the dead inside when he trained his torch on them: wide-eyed and agape. The smell of cordite and burning jet fuel wafting over everything as in the distance the town continued to ignite and erupt, spouting up gouts of red and flame. He reached the cockpit's windshield, marshaling extra caution, for it sloped dangerously down. The glass slick and precipitous. Inching in his slippers. Crouching gradually down, ever ever so slowly. Finally he chanced to shine the halogen beam inward. First, the co-pilot, seated as were the passengers, his head drooping as though now the harvest of a hangman's noose, and then the pilot in similar repose. And that's when he saw her. A flight attendant? Yes. Wedged beneath the pilot's seat and the curvature of the window behind her. Thrown there either by the force of the detonation or the force of the landing. The plastic remains of her former deployment scattered about: a plate scarred by food stains. A coffee cup that once sat on its saucer. A tray upon which she had borne this modest yet hallowed sustenance. But it was when he shone the full force of the halogen's brightness upon her face that she turned that face towards him—her dark eyes and thick raven of hair—turned her beautiful face towards him and looked square into his eyes. Who—or what?—are you? those eyes inquired. Death? My savior? Have—have you come for me? And Nial in shock and desperation sprang upright and doing so lost all control over his fragile footing and in fighting to regain it he fell backwards and down, his spine and head slamming in a brief second onto the unforgiving churchfield. As his breath and soul expired, his shade continued its journey beneath, perhaps landing in the sweet asphodel of the underworld, while in the world above, the town continued to burn and explode.

Postscript

(A few weeks later:
early January 1989, Vancouver, BC)

"A—a letter, love," Susan finally summoned the nerve to tell Roger, having fetched the mail many minutes before. "An aerogram from—from Scotland."

"Lockerbie?"

"Yes."

"Pam, no doubt. Hope she's coping."

"It's—it's not from Pam."

"Though how could she be—coping, I mean."

"I said, it's not *from* Pam."

"How could any of them be?"

"Love, it's not from Pam."

"What?"

"No."

"But—but it must be. I mean, who else?"

"It's—it's from Nial."

"Nial?"

"Yes."

"Don't have me on, love. It's not like you. That's almost cruel."

"I'd never. Never. It's—it *is* from Nial."

"But—but it can't be. He's—"

"It is, love. Postmarked the day before the—"

"The crash?"

"Yes."

POLO IN GAZA;

OR, A POEM OF LONGING

One

The summer that someone or some*thing* began cutting the heads and nipples off of females at the main campus (Gainesville) of the University of Florida,[11] Polo was offered a place in its graduate writing program. In those summer months he and Julie rented a walk-out basement apartment on Vancouver's North Shore, halfway to the summit of Grouse Mountain, passable-enough digs that they shared with their two sons, Griff and Andrew—four and three respectively. Polo had also won a seat in the University of Montana's grad program—his absolute first choice—but U Florida poet William Logan rang him one evening.

"The selection committee, and I agree wholeheartedly,

---

11. Daniel Harold "Danny" Rolling (aka the Gainesville Ripper) was arrested and charged with the murders and mutilations in November of 1991. The Missoula Police Department dispatched Detective Sims to Florida to ascertain if Rollins had any connection to the murder and mutilation of Riordan's daughter Christine but could not establish a firm connection. Rolling, convicted of the Florida murders, died from lethal injection in 2006.

thought your story aesthetically authentic. But the poems about the dead child."

"'God's Barbershop'? 'A Refusal to Mourn'?"

"Yes. The others on the evaluation committee thought them, well—"

"Derivative?"

"Of course, that. But also lacking a—a—"

"An objective correlative?"

"Exactly. We never see the poet face-to-face actually experience the loss of the child."

Silence. Face aflush, Polo clutched at words but grasped not a one. Not quite 9:00 p.m., the boys were tucked in bed and Julie confronted her final half hour as she manned the reference desk at the Edgemont branch of the North Van library.

"But the 'Runway' story," Logan told him, stabbing at some means to salvage the conversation, "well, quite the opposite. You—you had it published, right?"

"A shorter version."

"Yes. And I'd like to see you expand on it. On its cruel truths. Perhaps some kind of a novel. And do so here. At UF."

A silence ensued.

"Look," Logan told him, "you don't have to commit tonight. I just wanted to let you know the opportunity we're offering. Full tuition waiver and a not-too-shabbily-paid assistantship."

"Tuition waiver?"

"Full. And don't forget the assistantship. Teaching experience, remember. For getting a job after you graduate. But as I say, you don't have to commit tonight."

Polo paused. Finally he said:

"Sorry, Professor Logan," and skated past. "It's just that I—I just managed to get my two young sons settled down. When their mother's not here, they do all they can to stay awake until she gets home."

"Of course," Logan said. "I completely empathize." A pause. "So, nice hearing your voice. Bit of a trace of an accent," he said. "Brit?"

"Sí. I'll teach in RT," Polo observed.

Logan laughed, a short but warm and genuine one. "RT: Received Thespian. Good touch. Intimidate the bejeezus out of all of our thick-headed jocks." He fell silent. "About the poems," he said, "perhaps your, *their* subject is, well, too personal."

Polo allowed him to finish, guessing all too accurately Logan's next words:

"I think it was Eliot who said that the best way to forge your own heartbreak into art is to steal another's."

"Sounds like Eliot."

"That's our Thom. *Another's* heartbreak."

THUS DID HE BELLYACHE TO Julie when she arrived home:

"I felt—well, as a writer I'm not allowed to say the cliché word 'crestfallen'—but sort of, you know, hollowed out."

"Because you wanted something else," Julie said. They talked in the tiny basement kitchen: veneer cupboards, a twenty-inch avocado-green stove, a single-door harvest-gold reefer.

"I don't know that I'd say that," he countered.

She whupped open the fridge door and yinged down the

worthless plastic door to the cramped freezer compartment.
She poked about within.

"Everybody *always* wants something else," she said, "always.
Like me tonight. I want Marionberry Pie ice cream but all we
have is fucking vanilla."

"Griff's fave."

"Andrew's too."

She let the freezer compartment door scring closed and
whipped the fridge door across to shut. Braced her arms at full
extension by gripping the fridge door's upper gasket and gazed
down between those arms at the floor's vinyl tiling, in desperate search. "And—and I want a vodka-and-orange," she said.

"A screwdriver," he said.

"A vodka-and-orange," she repeated. "And then another."

Polo soothed her shoulder with his hand, squeezing it with
the gentlest of caresses.

"Don't," he said. "Okay? We've done this."

She turned her eyes upon his: emeralds in a moist sea of pale.

"And I want—"

"Don't, Jules, okay? Please?"

Now she narrowed those startling eyes, and she nodded
at him with no small fierceness and took a huge breath, tears
fountaining from her eyes and said:

"A vodka-and-orange."

"Can do."

"And—and," she said, and now she whispered the next ten
syllables as if each were biting off one of her fingers: "I want to
kiss my dead daughter good night."

·

"IT WAS THE TALISMAN," SHE said in some sunken hour before dawn.

He too was awake, the peace of sleep and dream long ago torn from them both like paper-doll's clothes.

"The shandy," she said.

"Jules, even The Swayze," he said, meaning Dr. Swayze, whom they'd both visited in the ear-splitting silence of the months-long aftermath. "Even he said that was impossible."

"It was the Talisman. The shandy."

"The shandy was at Casey's Road House."

"The Talisman," she repeated almost wordlessly. "Why— why did you choose that? Of all names. Of all places."

"Jules," he said, "go on, roll over. Go to sleep."

"Of all places."

THE CHILD'S SLIGHT AND DAMPENED soul hovered amongst them, at times like a chilling draught riven in beseech under their front door to creep square into each's ribcage, a crippling wind from each their own private underworld, and this it had done so for the five years since the child's death. Sometimes you could passage through hours or even days but then the next midday you yank open the IGA freezer door and reach in for a package of Stouffer's frozen lasagna and all you can hear and see—yes, "see," because it's that corporeal to you—all you can hear and see is that night's breathless silence that screams at you over your nine-month-old daughter's baby monitor.

W hen he chanced to brace the U.S.-Canadian border at Blaine, Washington, the U.S. border guard sneered at him (and this is no exaggeration):

"Where the hell d'ya think *you're* going?"

He was driving their '89 Subaru Justy, a tiny four-wheel-drive hatchback they had paid for with cash. His stuff relegated to the crawl space behind the front seats: his duffel-bagged clothes, his RadioShack computer (128K!), and his satchel of books: amongst them Dylan Thomas's *Selected Poems*; of course his treasured gift from atop his zafu, Roshi Aitken's haiku book, *A Zen Wave*; and what Polo dubbed his "Drowning Pool": Jim Harrison's *The Theory and Practice of Rivers* and James Wright's *Above the River*.

"Well?" the guard repeated.

"Florida," Polo answered the guard. "The university."

This was 4:37 a.m., and on this early morning back then in August 1990 Polo favored a closely cropped beard to offset his wisp-fine hair, which he similarly closely cropped. And thus these two grooming features, augmented by his genetically narrow face and his hours in the gym and his tan, well, strangers invariably assumed he was of the gay persuasion. A "fag," as they were then derisively tagged (amongst worse). This U.S. border official was no different:

"And what're you going to be doing down there?" the guard snarked. "As if I couldn't guess."

Polo frowned, then ceded to his truculent stubbornness, which was easily the guard's equal:

"Well," Polo told him, "I plan to suck every cock in Florida and when my belly's fuller with gism than Rod Stewart's, I'll drive back up here and suck yours."

"What the hell?"

"Oh. Did I say something untoward?"

"Jesus fuck. You people."

BUT THAT DIDN'T HAPPEN OF course. What really happened was this:

"Where the hell d'ya think *you're* going?"

"Florida. The university."

"And what're you going to be doing down there? As if I couldn't guess."

"Actually, since you ask, I'm going to earn my MFA by writing a series of elegiac devotionals in honor of my crib-death daughter."

This utterly blanched the border guard of anything even resembling a retort.

"Devotionals," Polo elaborated. "Poems of remembrance and loss. Haiku. Villanelles. Sestinas. Whatever my muse sends me."

"Your muse?"

"Shoshanna. My dead baby."

The guard stood silent and rigid as a pillar.

"Well?" Polo asked.

The guard hesitated then nicked his head Stateside.

"Cross over," he said.

BUT THAT DIDN'T HAPPEN EITHER, both previous variants spooling out only in Polo's slightly hungover upper-brainpan, a self-aggrandizement repeated constantly as he grindled down the Puget coast to then, in Seattle's booming downtown, pilot left and snare I-90's lanes east and inland, scaling the pass at Snoqualmie as the sun awoke and ignited his windshield with blood-orange glare. He flapped the visor down and stiffened erect in his seat like at the drive-in when dating a too-tall girl. He shouldered past semis and RVs and Thule-topped battered Subarus. A T-shirted guy in fringed lower leathers astride a Harley hog with ape-hangers, a worthless steel Wehrmacht helmet chin-strapped to his skull. Once across the pass and by mile marker fifty-six, he dipped the little hatchback down the eastern spine of the Cascades—Easton, Cle Elum, Ellensburg—then fought the severe crosswind at Vantage as he broached and bridged the sea-wide Columbia, rising in seek of the great river's eastern banks. Summiting and atop its upmost ridge, he commenced the eighty-mile-an-hour drift across the sage-brush and tumbleweed barrenness of the eastern Washington badlands (the true badlands—those of South Dakota—would he suffer twenty-four hours hence and which in comparison to these present ones he would pronounce to be Albion itself). Still, a tree-less, grass-less doldrum, a sunbaked unbroken expanse of blanched straw. He sailed by a fully leathered couple riding a Roadster, her arms encircling his waist, chunnering to each other via their headgear's microphones, a distraction from the monotony he pined for. Alas, though here and there the flatness would be broken by a moraine or esker, mild elevations around which the highway and Polo would snake only to re-enter once again the relentless flatness, the sunlight wincing and without respite. In contrast, Spokane in the early afternoon offered forth its cringing skyline like the city on the hill, a low-rent Omaha, and Polo flushed with rejuvenation. He crossed the Idaho border and fueled up in Coeur d'Alene. This was in 1990, so the Army Corps of Engineers had yet to complete construction of the towering viaduct over the Coeur d'Alene gorge. Thus, like all travelers he was diverted along the two-lane lakefront, the lake itself always a moment beyond his passenger-side window, a glittering sail-and-jet-ski throb of blue that made him mad with thirst and envy.

Back on I-90, in seeming seconds, he knifed the little hatchback across the Idaho panhandle, scaled the switchbacks of Lookout Pass and coasted down through the Rockies towards Missoula. A hundred-plus miles to go. Surrounded now by more and more Harleys. Convoys of them. Early August but back then he'd never heard of Sturgis, though he knew of the Black Hills from a Jim Harrison novel he'd read. The Sioux? Crazy Horse? A James Welch novel? The Harleys alternately entangled and spurned him, easy, aloof, oblivious. The beer-bellied *pudda-pudda* of their single-strokes like the accelerating rain of turnip and russet poured in steady measure from a bushel basket onto the lid of an empty washing machine.

Patented, they say.

Not so? Then otherwise listen to this (weeks earlier): a long-distance phone call: from North Vancouver to Missoula, Montana:

"English Department. This is Karen."

"Oh, hi, Karen. This—this is Alexander Polo. I've applied—ah, I'm an applicant to the graduate writing program."

"Yes, you have, and yes, you are. And I just a few moments ago finished typing your acceptance letter."

"Acceptance? Really?"

"I tell no lies."

"Geez, that's bloody wonderful. Just bloody wonderful. 'Scuse my French."

"No excuses needed. It'll be in the system mail by tomorrow. It's summer so we only have one round of department pickups."

"That's okay."

"Be at the post office Sunday night."

"Great. Just great."

"Anything else?"

"Well, yes. Ah, along with the acceptance, did I get ah, you know, an assistantship? A TA?"

"Let me look. Your letter's near the top of my pile."

"That's okay, Karen, really."

"Nonsense. You want to know, don't you?"

He didn't answer. Rather, he *couldn't* answer.

"Here it is. Mr. Polo? You still there?"

"Still."

She paused. She sighed. "Sorry," she said, "but I'm not seeing an offer. Of a TA."

The truth invariably renders us mute and this one so rendered Polo. The department secretary too had no words. Until these:

"They do cite in the letter the strength of your submissions."

"My poems."

She fell silent.

"Look," she said, "don't let this discourage you. More than one or two TA-less grad students have come here and subsequently earned a full ride. I could give you names, but I'd be violating federal law."

"My poems."

"Actually, the letter uses the words 'your poetry.'"

"My poetry."

"Yes. I'm sorry. About the other."

"Don't be, Miss Karen. I'm not."

But he was—he fucking-well was.

A h, but the non-haiku triumvirate of books in his satchel: Thomas and Wright and Harrison. Also gifts from Julie. From the North Van library's donation table. Each she had spirited in her locker in the employees' break room until, of all evenings, Winter Solstice, when she fêted him with all three at once.

He considered the books priceless, a treasure beyond measure, their covers as hand-worn as their inner pages were immaculate and sacred. On that solstice night he passed through the trio a dozen times without breaching those covers, as if taking and giving communion at once. Wafers of the gods. Tropes of their querents.

"But which should I read first?" he said.

She thought for a moment.

"Ask—ask Shoshe," Julie replied. "Shoshanna."

Over their inter-bedroom intercom, you could actually hear the child wet its diaper. Hear the child's dreaming. Its hope, its trust, its prayer. You could hear all that, but on that night you could not hear the child's heart skip a beat, then skip another, then paw desperately in her crib at her bedclothes, then sink silently, quietly, and evermore into death. What you could hear and would hear till end of days was her gasping last breaths, her clutching at the short months of life here on Earth, the clear echoing note of your unremitting anguish.

The rows of motionless Harleys glinted in the parking lot moonlight like the pale and still ghosts of the Age of Machines, an age long passed. He stood at the window of this room in the Livingston, Montana, Best Western, sipping from a tin of Oly. Falsely self-congratulatory: for he had sworn to himself (and Julie) to *not* stop in Missoula; to not there visit the campus of the university; to not stand before the Liberal Arts building that skirted the north sector of the grassy quadrant, its lush and wavering maples; to not conjure the English Department inside; to not call forth its blind bastards that had offered him meager acceptance but no financial ride whatsoever; to not curse and damn them all, curse and damn them all for days' time gone and all days' time to come.

The child was born as quickly as a sneeze, whoojing down Jules's birth canal like a pup in a waterslide. She touched Earth boasting sky-blue eyes and angel-white hair (which promptly fell out, rendering the little pudding as delectably chrome-domed as a nascent pearl). She smiled and laughed incessantly ("Er, that's actually just gas, Zandy."), and when at six months she sat up and started to crawl, she pinwheeled in her jammies across the hardwood floors and Persian carpets of their loft like—like:

"A lariat," he whispered to Julie.

"In footies," Julie added.

But it was the child's laughter—and it *was* laughter. Don't believe me? Then listen, and you can hear her as Polo does now in that godforsaken hotel room in Livingston, Montana, hear her as he tickles her and blows flatulent noises on the immaculate perfection of her bellyflesh. Come, listen to the beautiful Shoshanna as she giggles:

"Eee-iy! Ha ha!"
Vooreeet!
"Ha ha ha!"
"Zandy!"
"What?"
"That's kind of—"
"Kind of what?"
"I don't know—gross?"
Vooreet.

He stretched the next day's drive into ten hours, blazing west past the up-yours refinery stacks in Billings, Montana, and hammering south (still on I-90) past the Custer Monument in Crow Agency, the topography at least rolling and somewhat distinct but the vegetation pale and sapped, the stalks stooped as a convalescent, more grasshopper than grass. An hour later, shut of Montana and skirting Sheridan, Wyoming, he scoffed down three Egg McMuffins and a sixteen-ounce cauldron of scalding colored water that the breakfast board misnomered as coffee, and after filling his other tank (the one in the Justy), he tried on a "King Ropes" ball cap at the Exxon C-store. Teal peak and panel; a brilliant mesh crown.

I grew up dreamin'
of bein' a cowboy . . .

Beside the ball cap inventory was nailed to the laminate an aluminum mirror and in its grimed distortion Polo took stock of himself: gaunt and scruff, more tenement vagrant than ranch hand, the cap perched atop his nog like some woebegone mallard. Would Shoshe've looked like him? Been like him? Worthless? Resigned? Defeated? He stood here in the middle of a C-store in the middle of nowhere bound for nowhere else, a daft and mocking cowpoke of a yarmulke on his head, the moment a bitter pause in a two-thousand-mile furtherance to the humidity of where he didn't want to go.

No one ever gets what they want.

Never?

They do cite in the letter how they admired your poetry.

My poems?

Yes.

Yeah? Well obviously they admired'm not fucking enough. Well, they can go bark up a dead horse's arse.

He paid $6.99 for the hat and $29.99 for a room in the Best Western in Pierre, South Dakota, collapsing after a horrific flight across the true badlands. A vile and blank topography, a snow-blindness without respite of and without snow, an uninterrupted and eye-wincing nothingness save the occasional squalor: Rapid City; a hundred thousand roadside Wall Drug signs staved in the parched soil like an endless parade of craven realtor signs. Each and all signifying nothing. Indeed, motoring across that replenished barrenness, he thought not of the topography of our arid moon but the life-drained cliffs of

Uranus or Pluto. If the glaciers had not ten millennia earlier scraped clean any morsel of gravid topsoil, surely the Bureau of Indian Affairs back in the nineteenth century would've quashed and commandeered nature's recalcitrance. Scraping the earth clean with gargantuan steam-driven bulldozers, ones powered by coal and belching billows of black smoke, all before sentencing what remained of the Plains Indians to their lifeless and infertile reservations, there to huddle in their pox-tainted blankets as they awaited the final implementation of the bureau's genocide.

Musings gleaned from an undergraduate sociology class he no doubt had slept-in on or otherwise told to bugger off.

And of course: ever the roaring horde of bikers. Back then in the early 1990s they were still burly and unredeemable, sleeveless and tattooed Visigoths who had not yet traded in their ape-hanger hogs for flaccid three-wheel roadsters and social security checks. Still a swarming horde of brute and barbarity, all thundering forth with strut and disdain to their Black Hills mecca, its deafening percussional lifting Polo in his stubby little jam-jar of a car to God knew where. But it seemed God wasn't telling—at least not for a few more days.

Road warriors face but two choices when staring down the road's dark and endless nights: the shared loneliness of the lounge or the haunted emptiness of their room: six of one, a half-empty dozen of the other. Just ask our own frayed warrior: Polo the Lost. This night, after a porterhouse steak in the hotel dining hall (wilted asparagus, baked potato in its jacket with sour cream and chives), Polo pinned his declining spirits on the latter. He steadily lowered the level of his restaurant bottle of pinot noir and slumped in the bedside armchair, to the muted wane of the bed light and the past.

Earlier in the day in Rapid City just over the Wyoming–South Dakota border, he'd refueled at a Shell mega-station, the trucks and Harleys whomping past yards from him in blistering welts. The blast furnace entryway to hell's interstate. A crushing reality. And now here in his Pierre, South Dakota, hotel room he wormed his spine and backside deeper between the arms of the chair and deeper and deeper into his resentment and despair. I mean, what the fuck? Is this what he came for? Lived on this earth for? His lot for time to come?

And then in the vileness of that Rapid City superstation with the petroleum fumes and heat woozying him, he was paid a visit by an angel. Though Polo wouldn't recognize the angel as such until years hence. A battered Cadillac hearse—from its tail fins a late-1950s relic—gunned up to the pump behind his tidy gnome of a hatchback. Paint-blistered. All the windows down. Formerly vinyl roof peeled to steel by the sun like a scalped grape.

Inside a dark and molten freight of teens and children, and they swarmed over each and every other to secure first purchase to the world beyond the hearse's spavined doors. The doors burst open, and entwined like the gush of a waterwheel they tumbled out. A few adults. One teen carrying a baby. Quite remarkable, their hair glistening and wavy and succulent as plums, all laughing and jubilant as holidayers, all seeking the soft drink coolers and candy counters, the toilets and air conditioning in the C-store inside. They laughed and poked at each other and mocked the others of their troupe in Spanish.

"No hay chocolate para ti, hermano. A las chicas no les gustan las espinillas."

"Salvo a las que tienen sus propias, hermanita."[12]

And then he noticed. From the front passenger seat an old man was watching him—no, studying him. Polo switched his

12. "No chocolate for you, big brother. The girls do not like pimples."
"Except those that have their own, little sister."

attention back to his task, brimmed up the tank, withdrew the fuel nozzle, secured the cap, flapped close the cover with his elbow, and clinched nozzle and handle back into their berth in the pump.

When Polo turned back to his car the old man was standing not a few feet from him. Thin. Utterly silent. All manner of weather and world on that dark and ancient face. White and silvered hair in a reed down his back, woven in braids tight as a hawser. Laundered-to-gray Hanes T-shirt. Knobble-kneed jeans. And of all things brand-new high-topped white sneakers. Chuck Taylors. Immaculate. As if he'd moments before unboxed them from their lidded encasement. The old man gestured at Polo's rear license plate.

"Estás lejos de casa, amigo, muy lejos."[13]

Polo stood puzzled. As a sophomore in his Toronto high school over twenty-five years earlier, he'd bumbled through a semester of Spanish before switching to Latin for his language elective (Français was mandatory). The old man never skipped a note. He nodded his head towards the C-Store, speaking rapidly:

"Los niños. En ocasiones me vuelven loco. ¿Pero en otros? Son como mariposas."[14] Pensive, he returned his attention to Polo.

"¿Hacia dónde te diriges? ¿Este? ¿Oeste?"[15]

---

13. You are far from home, my friend, very far.
14. The children. At times they drive me crazy. But at others? They are like butterflies.
15. Where are you headed? East? West?

"Sorry? I—I don't speak Spanish."

The old man squinted at him and tilted his head, both sage and befuddled, like an Inuit ancient led to his ice floe. "Los niños," he said once more, "mariposas," and like a Yaqui sorcerer he was soundlessly and miraculously gone. As if evaporated.

Now in his hotel room this night in Pierre, South Dakota, with the past and eternity wrapped around him like his own pox-infected blanket, Polo doubted the entire encounter. The petroleum fumes? The isolation? The fatigue? His single-semester Spanish had rendered him only three words in translation: "niños," "loco," "otros": "baby," "crazy," "others." Jesus fuck. Well, four, actually, but "amigo" didn't count, i.e., he'd never swotted Hindi but as a kid he'd scootched his arms and legs into "pajamas" every night and dog-paddled himself awake every morning in his bedroom in his parents' "bungalow."

Niños, loco, otros. Baby, crazy, others. Shite! When would it end? Never?

He shook his head to slough off the bureau's blanket and with a flex of his triceps he clambered up out of the chair, battling back his reverie. He would work. Draft a poem. At least its nascence. *They do cite in the letter the strength of your poetry.* Pouring the last of the pinot into the plastic hotel tumbler, he skinned from his suitcase his wear-worn satchel and from within it his crude and spoken tools: watermarked twenty-four-pound linen paper, unlined, in wait of his; his cherished box of Eberhard Faber Blackwing 602 pencils, each one pre-sharpened, the slender cedar of its wood polished into a pearlescent blue, the iconic flattened crimp of the eraser ferrule.

But why would the old geez assume he spoke Spanish? His King Ropes cap? His dark tan beneath? His itinerance (all his worldly possessions in his car)? Seeking inspiration, he shunted aside his Thomas and Harrison and discovered that Julie had secreted inside yet another of her gifts: this too a book: a slender volume and wrapped in plain white tissue paper as thin as a prayer. Inside that sacred tissue? A chapbook: *Twenty Love Poems and a Song of Despair.* By Pablo Neruda. The translations by G. H. LeGue. Who? Obviously yet again from the library's donation table. How had he stumbled on this woman? His love. The mother of his sons. His daughter.

Yes, his dead daughter. He sipped his wine. Flipped through the poems. Neruda's originals in Spanish facing the English translations. "Para que tú me oigas"—"So that you will hear me." "Casi fuera del cielo"—"Almost out of the sky." Who the fuck was G. H. LeGue? "Me gustas cuando callas"—"I like it when you whisper." To wit:

> *I like it when you whisper*
> *For I can hear you in your absence.*

The words stopped him. Fuck. How deafeningly could he hear her? Shoshe? Hear her now—a thousand miles and a thousand years of tears later. Jesus. And then he made the lethal mistake of reading on:

> *Dream, my butterfly. You are my soul,*
> *You are my sadness.*

•

DREAM, MY BUTTERFLY.

That night he'd awoken, alone in their bed. Loco. A silence that pierced his eardrums as definitively as if they had been hilted by knitting needles.

No, the old bugger had pointed to his license plates: British Columbia: Columbia? Colombia? Sí, Colombia.

For a spilt-second back on that night he remained hidden in their bed, the prescience of the forthcoming horror like a concrete slab across his chest, his soul, his heart. And then the cowardice of reluctance and next the unmanageable and sulfuric stench of his own terror and sweat.

Como mariposas? Of course: They are like butterflies. Children.

A swallow of pinot. Fuck and double fuck. He stood at the hotel room window. Its drapes, each as heavy as a radiology apron, he swept apart. The topography beyond? Dark bleakness backlit, as if the moon now shone from beneath the earth's crust. For next you are afloat, like some unsprung cloven vessel, swamped and in drift on chartless seas, floundering down the hallway to your daughter's nursery.

And now, mate, such as you are, you stand in her doorway, ex-paperboy father, ruddled and in ruin, and such as you are do you behold in the darkness the sight of your child and her mother: Julie, ashiver and bone-naked, her bare skin a horrifying and translucent blue: she clasping the swaddled Shoshanna to her breast, clasped there as if in wan nourish, and both mother and child ghost-washed by the window's pale sheaf of moonlight.

"They have stolen our child," she tells you in a hushed voice.

How many moments elapse? A thousand? Ten thousand? How many before you whimper:

"Jules? Julie?"

"You heard me," she says in that same voice: possessed by the deafening hush from beyond. "God—fucking *God*—has stolen our childe."

BUT AVERT NOT YOUR EYES, Alexander. For now: See the dead child: no longer a swaddling but older and standing at a window, one that looks out beyond a railing and a deck and farrows down through the hedges (rose of Sharon) and scattered flowers (mock orange). Beyond this vegetation stretches the sand, wimpled and sodden and which frames jagged outcroppings that thrust forth from the sea, barely a league hence. Black as anthracite and clustered like an island. Utterly barren and now as always locked in battle with the white foam of the waves. In the house a figure now hovers beside the child, the outside landscape and seascape eerily visible through his silhouette.

Are—are we ghosts, Poeta? she asks.

Sombra. We are shades.

The room they inhabit is partitioned here and there by free-standing shelves cluttered with marine decanters of all manner of shape and color, some reflecting the morning light like dancing flames, others the evening light like choirs of smoke. On a countertop, a ship in a bottle awaits patiently within its glass berth. A masthead nearby stands watch like a quelled and silenced furie incased in an eternity of wood.

My father mourns for me, Poeta.

The world mourns for you.

In that room time passes not, yet nor does it pause; it exists yet exists not, like a blink of a blind eye. Thus now does La Poeta turn to her and hold out a translucent hand. The child takes it, and without any movement whatsoever the two stand seaward by twin graves where the vegetation breaches the beach.

Matilde Urrutia. Pablo Neruda.

The graves not covered by grass nor moss nor age but by sand so pure it could engender the goblets that held the wine of that final supper near Gethsemane. The sand immaculate save for a single dome of green dianthus that crouches by the headstones like a charmed hedgehog and at the foot of the graves by the flowering lips of sweet william so pink they might yet be kisses.

See? The dead too mourn for you.

She looks at the gravestones.

Even the dead grieve?

How—how could they not?

She waits, struggling to compose her next utterance.

What—what will I tell him, Poeta? My papa?

My butterfly, you already have.

In the stricken dawn, with the shadows of the Dakota hills spreading towards him like the leprous hands of the same God who stole his child, Polo drove due east on his unchosen course to confront that God, and when by midday, sapped and dispirited, he eased back the throttle and stilled, he bivouac'd his little craft to the side of the great highway and with both passenger's-side windows rolled down for circulation and both driver's-side windows rolled up for survival, he slept. Not yards from his sleeping head, the semi-trucks whomped by him in a ceaseless stream, the shock waves of their ensuing turbulence battering and torsioning the hatchback like a cradle in a treetop. But this bough breaketh not, and as he slept, those hands of God—the mere shadows of the hills as some might think—when those shadowed hands passed directly over him at high noon they—as all gods eventually do—vanished, but not before was there writ in the blanched and desiccated sand for him to see upon awakening: a lariat just like the night at

The Talisman, but this lariat crafted not of snowflakes but of butterflies: pure. white. butterflies.

AFTER AN ETERNAL MOMENT OF awe and contemplation, Polo turned his little car around and headed back the way he came: west, following those butterflies—and Shoshanna.

Intermezzo

The world, as Saint Paul in Corinthians II is too oft misquoted, suffers not fools gladly. Let us herein exalt the fools because that same world suffers would-be poets even less gladly, as Polo, after over a decade of rejections of his odes, and his elegies and laments, could attest. True, over those years he published a few pieces of quirky journalism and personal essays ("From AAA to Zzyyton: Teaching Your Sons to Effortlessly Tear the L.A. Phone Book in Half," and "Sorry, Argentina, but You Had It Wrong About Grief: One Nail (Un Clavo) Does *Not* Drive Out Another (Otro Clavo)." These and a few others were enough to ballast his ectomorph vitae to secure him a series of ill-paid and untenured lectureships at a variety of community colleges in the Pacific Northleft—North Idaho in Coeur d'Alene; Skagit in Mount Vernon, Washington; and Edmonds in Edmonds, Washington—but his many applications for tenure-track positions met the same wall of disdain and indifference as his elegies and laments.

But then, in March of 2009, on a day almost equidistant between Barack Obama's inauguration and the twenty-fifth anniversary of the child's death, he received an anonymous parcel in the mail that in his career as a poet wrought if not a sea change then "a bit of bloody all right," as will he tell us in his own words and in a few moments.

But first, Riordan and his immortal love Béatrize: Bea: though now she lies dying.

LOS VIOLINES

One

Double-clutching and down-gearing, Riordan gunned the two-seater Triumph sharp right from the main drag (Higgins) onto South Third, and there in a fleeting instant he saw the sandwich board on the sidewalk outside Shakespeare & Co:

County Commish Bea Tully Sims
Dying here from her cancer
Leiomyosarcoma
This Friday
7:00 p.m.

Another double-clutch and down-gear and he shiv'd the little sports car into one of the diagonal parking stalls across from the bookstore, the four-cylinder engine's deep-throated growl softening to a purr as he braked and switched off the ignition.

He'd lost weight since Bea's remission had proven to be illusory—too much weight, she complained—and he yinged open the car door and with his hands offering aid spidered his long legs—lank as an empty pair of coveralls—out from under the steering wheel and across the threshold of the rocker panel. He stood. His footing on the dry asphalt of the roadbed a tad unsteady. The impending death of your beloved? Your immortal? He'd had the top down in today's warmth and sunshine and he *thoonk'd* the car door shut behind him and squinted in the shimmering glare to stare down and defy the portents of the sandwich board. And stare them down he did. For which portents were in reality thus:

U of M grad and Seattle U faculty Alexander Polo
Reading here from his poetry chapbook
Death and the Butterfly
This Friday
7:00 p.m.

"You, Jack? A reading?"

He *fwapped* her gently across the hip. His other hand held the syringe at the end of his upright forearm like a conductor his baton, a syringe which he now primed, the tiny spurt of morphine sulfate (15 mg/ml) evaporating into their bedroom's air-conditioned air—he was *that* practiced. "Come on," he said, "roll over."

Lying on the bedsheets, Bea did so, tugging down the waist elastic of her pajama bottoms with her thumbs as she twisted, a graceful balletic that had once filled him with dizzying lust but now underscored for him the day of the month. The month of the year. Each day seemingly shorter than its other before.

There. He studied the flesh of her backside. Far too much of it pitted with these microscopic starfish bruises.

"I mean, a *poetry* reading, Jack? You?"

On the bedside table was a petri dish of alcohol and beside it a cotton swab. With his hand not holding the syringe, he swabbed a patch of her still-beautiful rump and prepared to inject her.

"I thought we could go together," he said.

"To the reading?"

"No. To Isla Negra."

"Where?"

"A beach. In Chile. Where Neruda lived."

"Neruda?"

She looked at him—no, she stared, startled and marveled. Alas, no opiate exists to dull the pain of foresight—that of loss to come—and he could see how much her eyes ached, ten-fold more than the besieged tissues of her flesh.

"My markwiss," she managed. "We could buy a, you know, a motor coach?"

"Nah," he said. "We'll take the Triumph."

BACK IN HIGH SCHOOL IN Butte, those five incomprehensible decades ago—Thalidomide, Sputnik, the Salk vaccine—they claimed you could start on U.S. 93 at the Canadian-Montana border and drive all the way down to the tip of South America without ever making a left turn. Or a right. The same road. Descending the globe of the hemisphere like sectioning with your thumbs a lush and peeled orange. Was that so? Riordan liked the sheer simplicity of such a notion, liked it so much that he'd never investigated the claim for its veracity. Besides, what of it? He'd a decade ago sold the motor coach without it ever breaching the city's limits. True, he suffered the $11K loss with a bit more than a grumpy shrug but as well as salvaging the twin BC license plates (cleated to a beam-post in his garage by his workbench) and selected content of the driver's console (the poems, the letters, the "Runway" article), he siphoned off a few thou of the leftover money to buy the Triumph motorcar, a TR4A, one that he'd meticulously restored. Walnut dash. Dual Stromberg carbs that he supercharged. The steering wheel sheathed in a kid-leather chap.

All pointless—perhaps.

For now here he sat on their deck high in the South Hills, the town below him miniature in the afternoon light and ac-rawl like a colony of gentrified ants. In contrast, in the distance stood the jagged Bitterroots, motionless as Grenadiers and blue as ice caps. Speaking of ice caps, he'd taken to drinking ice wine, perfect here in these blazing summer months. He quite fancied the gewürztraminer from Canada, but he occasionally paired that off with a Washington State chenin blanc. He also wouldn't turn down an ice-cold Bud Light Lime if you spotted him one, especially while he Weber'd New Zealand rib chops as he planned on for this evening's supper. All of this pointless elaboration. When Bea's pestilent sarcoma had heartbreakingly returned, desperate for distraction, he'd enrolled in a cooking class at the Good Food Store (the local and more leftish incarnation of Whole Foods) but had dropped out after the first evening because of the missionary earnestness of his classmates: paleo-vegans and gluten-free omni's, whereas he just wanted to learn how to build a better Reuben. But next? Well, clothes were verboten because Bea had once outfitted him with the taste and aplomb of a Nordstrom's Head Buyer (the markwiss, remember?). So Riordan tried shoes, plunking down 347 dineros for a pair of calfskin Gucci loafers but of course he couldn't bear the guilt that they spurred in him. Imagine the calf's mother, shorn of her offspring for nothing more than to furnish elaborate footwear to bewildered old buggers in J-pressed slacks. Absurd.

Now, on this day in early autumn 2012, at the age of seventy-five, he wore Kmart flip-flops and khaki shorts. A faux Hawaiian shirt. He was, in a word, lost. Lost, but—and this is important—he also had a poetry reading to attend.

Two

It was titled *Death and the Butterfly* and subtitled *Nerudian Sonnets of Love and Deprivation by a Dead Airman as Whispered to Alexander Polo* and Riordan fell in love with its author, the Polo bloke, the moment he saw him. He topped a shade under six feet, was clean-shaven with a thin ruggedly square-jawed face and Riordan was smitten even more so when he heard him:

"Two decades ago, the poet William Logan, who also teaches at the University of Florida, told me that the truest way to write about your pain and loss was to write about the pain and loss of others. Of course, I didn't listen."

A faint but detectable Brit accent. In which accent, Polo continued:

"A few years later while I was here in UM's grad program, Bill Kittredge told me the same thing. I still didn't listen.

"Pigheaded and bullheaded, I tirelessly churned out elegies and eulogies and refusals-to-mourn the death by smiles of a child in footies. Of my child, my baby: Shoshe: Shoshanna. Imagine: All of it deemed by my professors and peers baleful, derivative dreck. A verdict repeated endlessly by a subsequent sea of editors, all justifiably so.

"Ah, but Shoshe. Shoshe died of SIDS—crib death, the preferred and more brutal term—and it still seems so—so fleeting. And yet, and yet . . ."

He paused. And here Riordan, hounded relentlessly by all existence, slid into his solar plexus—his soul at least. Jack. Jack? You there? What can you hear? What can you see? Your own child? Missing for seventy-two hours? You, your then wife sleepless? In famine? The prison of your modest house on the north side by the rail yard and switching tracks? Or another prison? The oncologist's office, a few months now past. The doctor with phrenology charts on his walls and an Eastern European accent. Kucharski. Dr. David. But unlike those years ago you do see these details for thief time had not yet robbed your third eye of its vision: the doctor, heavyset, silver-haired, strikingly handsome— "Like Cary Grant," Bea said.

"And then," the Polo bloke continued, "after all those failed poems and towering letters of rejection, I received in the mail a string-tied parcel. Postmarked Missoula, Montana. Plain brown wrapper. No return address. Like mail-order prurience. But inside—inside?"

He paused.

And our man Jack—as handsome as any Hugh or Cary, Grant or otherwise—sees another oncologist's office or, rather, its fleeting departure: this of Bea's initial diagnosis, four years before: "All the X-rays and tests point to, well, leiomyosarcoma. Uterine cancer." Who had that oncologist looked like? Unknown, save his hooded but empty robe, his menacing scythe.

"You see, I was in the badlands, of South Dakota," Polo related, "and I stopped at this gas station on I-90, and this old man—I fashioned him a Yaqui sorcerer—well he—he asked me questions in Spanish. He had mistaken my license plates to be from Colombia. And he said that children were like—well, it doesn't matter now. But back to that brown-wrapped parcel tied with string—I mean, who ties parcels with string anymore?—inside were blue aerograms and the pages from the magazine of my first sale. I'd written that piece about these plane-watchers up in Vancouver, Canada, eating their lunches at the end of the runway, watching as the incoming flights whooshed overhead and with their landing gears extended, reached like Adam's Sistine hands for the sanctuary of the earth."

But Riordan, poor sod, was still adrift within that initial diagnosis—that had poleaxed Riordan, though Bea disdained it as if it were a tiresome cold she hadn't quite yet shaken. In contrast, Riordan teetered through those ensuing months as if he was emotionally duckwalking, and one January day after driving Bea home from chemo and tucking her into the couch, snug with a goose-feather duvet, a quilt pillow, and a back-scratcher (against the skin-crawling side-effect of the chemo), he had fled to the haven of their double garage, to the cold certainties of his machinery: His workbench: coupled planks adzed from young Japanese chestnut, unlacquered, the grain specifically selected because of its legendary resistance to cold and moisture (Bea had by spousal edict forbidden a heated garage). To the workbench's side: his Redline toolbox, its sixteen drawers tiered like a Mayan temple. And in the twin bays: the 4A, a growly chunk of royal blue, and beside it Bea's sleek black Chrysler 300 sedan—essentially a four-door limousine—but its cab-forward design making it seem a great steel cat in crouch, a dark shadow of predation, at once territorial yet unbounded.

And PNM 103. The BC license plates cleated to the post between the sports car and the sedan and these brought him back to the poet:

"Along with the aerograms," the Polo bloke continued, "poems. Of Neruda's. On tissue-thin blue letter pad and transcribed in fountain ink. In a hand as beautiful as—as though the writer had employed not pen and ink but ink and brush. Poems she was studying. That she'd copied out.

"And so," Polo resumed, "I eventually came to the realization that everyone else was right and I was wrong—dreadfully and as always wrong—and so finally I sought to express my pain and grief over my beautiful baby daughter through the pain and grief of those sad four others."

And he cleared his throat and sipped his pinot gris, taking a few deep breaths, readying to recite.

As for Riordan, it was the sight of those license plates: *they* had impelled him to send his cache of the lettered remains of those four lives to the man—now a poet—who stood before him. The good Captain Robert had easily and readily tracked Polo down in Edmonds, Washington. And Riordan, fatally attached since Bea's diagnosis to the absurdly sentimental, had parceled them up within the folksong brown wrapping of his boyhood and—just as his father and his aunts and uncles would do to send their parcels to and from Butte, Montana, and County Cork—he tied and knotted them with unbleached twine.

And Polo—the recipient of that rough yet holiest of gifts—did now recite:

> *I Do Not Love You*
> *I do not love you like deserts love the night*
> *or rivers love the fealty of their banks.*

Riordan felt him pause momentarily before continuing:

> *I love you like violins love windows*
> *that open onto orchards and pear blossoms.*

As Polo recited the sonnet's final ten lines and the two or three sonnets that followed, Riordan, having danced atop those first four lines albeit with two left feet, nodded and thought, Violins. Really. Hmn.

"To Bea," Riordan told the Polo bloke when he presented the copy of the poems to be signed.

Polo eyed him. "To Bea—or not to be," he said, devoid of any flippance. "As in Beatrice?"

"Sí," Riordan answered.

Thus did our poet so inscribe and then sign his name with a flourish; but also, Riordan thought, with the gravitas of a man chiseling his epitaph into his own gravestone: for all and evermore to see.

He handed the slender chapbook to Riordan. About to speak, he instead searched Riordan's face. Riordan flinched. Averted his eyes. Perhaps a diversion to delay detection—ask him about the violins? Was that even allowed at these do's? Musings all pointless, for Riordan knew he was sussed.

"It—it was you, wasn't it," Polo said. A declarative rather than interrogative.

Riordan didn't respond. They studied each other. Two men: honesty and honor their shared tithe. And sadness.

"She's not well," Riordan said. "Bea. She—she would've come."

Polo nodded. He paused.

"Love the shirt," he finally said. "Hawaii?"

"Goodwill," Riordan said.

Three

She was sleeping. He set the inscripted chapbook atop the chestnut workbench in the garage and in the house he paid the RN for her time and stood beside her bedside and watched her. She slept sometimes for days—well, not days exactly but it seemed like it to him: so quiet that in terror he would put his ear to her breast to hear her heartbeat (he mistrusted his medical skills to find a pulse). On this evening, he drew up the replica Queen Anne chair that she so loved and sat and held her hand. Warm with life but then not. As if the blood now slowed in her veins. Her heart conserving her moments. That it had gathered. Hoarded.

A while passed.

"D'you—d'you know what my favorite day is?" he eventually and softly asked. "Of all the-Jack-and-the-Bea-Stalk's days? My favorite? When you won. Remember? In '02?"

•

THAT ELECTION NIGHT—that second-most humorless of decades earlier—they were scheduled to watch the returns in the ballroom of the downtown Holiday Inn. Metz had opted for a run at the U.S. Senate and the Dems had persuaded Bea to abandon her Independent tag and run on their ticket, an option she at first resisted—testing their sincerity—and then embraced.

"Killer Bea's," he said in toast as they prepared to leave the house.

"The mar-*kwiss*," she teased back.

"Of Avingdon," he added.

"Mmm," she agreed. She wore a Belgian linen pant suit, one of pale white, and a lavender silk camisole beneath. "The cami so I don't channel Hillary," she quipped. Back then the then senator from New York's name could be uttered without its withering baggage of irony and self-consciousness, and back then Riordan took Bea's hand in both of his and said:

"Mrs. Clinton'd be honored, Mrs. Riordan." He kissed her cheek.

"Tonight, I'm back to being Ms. Tully Sims, I'm afraid."

"Fine with me," he told her. "Besides, you don't have to be. At least not for the next half hour." He gave her cheek another kiss.

"Careful, Jack, I just might consider it. And you had exactly *what* in mind?"

"Patagonia? Machu Picchu? A trip through the Panama Canal?"

Which trip they did hasten through though still they

arrived late to the Holiday Inn and, amidst the dreary national returns, watched as CNN's regional feed had announced Bea's victory within an hour after the closing of the polls. Riordan had ensured a magnum of Taittinger's on hand, which they poured into Stuart crystal flutes and toasted in private and as thus:

"No more Killer Bea's," he said, raising the flute. "To the queen Bea."

Four words said on that night and said again this night these ten years later.

IN THE MORNING, HE AWOKE to find that he'd slept in his clothes beside her with his arm draped around her waist as though in clamor for her retention—but indeed she was gone.

Four

T he dead in their graves dissolve slowly, a freckle, a follicle, a cuticle at a time. Their grievers—still ambulant though as numb—dissolve even more so. Over the months he tried everything—his ravaged heart alternately longed for her flesh's return or for her ghost's precipitous dispatch—but no potion nor balm ceded him either. He visited the bookstore—Shakespeare & Co—but could only hear as he browsed through the shelves, "You, Jack? A reading?" He visited the council chamber where she wielded both gavel and mace and from which she had forbade his presence. ("I'll feel self-conscious. Like you're watching me in the shower." "But I do watch you in the shower.") The Good Food Store, site of his scowlingly truncated culinary tutelage. ("Jack, honey, it's only a cooking class. No one's expecting you to have play dates.")

Near New Year's he stood in his closet—their walk-in, actually—with a scrimped allotment of hanger space granted to those clothes she had bought him. Shirts and slacks and neckties. True skeletons. Each and every that she had scrupulously selected. For instance, this: a sky-blue Oxford-cloth button-down complemented by a dusty-rose-colored knitted tie: "As though you stepped right out of Burke's Peerage," she had pronounced when he first wore it. "You could stand for Parliament in that." "Parliament"—as opposed to "Congress." "Of course," she had laughed, "my beloved Jack will sully it with an uncivilized tie clip"—but he hadn't, hadn't sullied it. Nor her. Not even a once.

Naive? Sentimental? As an engineering major at Montana State back in the 1950s he had been pressed upon to read Schiller's famed essay on poetry in his sole and required English literature class. These years later he couldn't tell you. Nor of this: How, a few weeks later, on the coldest day of the year—spindrift frost heaving in clouds above the groaning pavements—clad only in his faux-Hawaiian getup, he screeched the Triumph backwards out of the garage, slammed the gear stick into first and with the top down roared the 4A down the mountainside, twisting the steering wheel back and forth with crossed forearms as he swooped down through the switchbacks, double-clutching and down-gearing, his feet and his hands in a fierce processional, the chunky motorcar whooshing like a luge through the frozen crystalline air. "Fuck yis!" he did scream into the curdling Montana winds as in the Triumph's cockpit he devoured the hairpins, the engine growling, roaring, less lion than wounded infuriated beast. "Fuck yis all!"

Eventually, as darkness rose, he recanted and retraced his descent in a more guarded invasion back home. The twin beams of his headlamps like prowler's flashlights. His face a Zhivago of ice.

In their kitchen he made chamomile with honey. He measured two tablespoons of Hennessey therein—no, make that three—and sat recovering in her recliner, streaming vintage Warner Bros. cartoons through her Roku onto their flat-screen as she used to. "The one where they die, Jack." "Huh?" "Bugs and Elmer." "They die?" "'The Old Grey Hare.' At the Butte Motor-Vu. Back in '54. Before *The High and the Mighty.*" "Christ, you're right. I was what—seventeen?" "Just find it." "Jesus. Seventeen. Dad's convertible." "Was—was she pretty?" "A Merc. A Monterey. A '53." "Well, was she?" "She—she was from Catalan."

Ah, but the cartoon: Elmer, a gray and wizened old man, finally fells Bugs with a rocket bazooka—this taking place in the far-in-the-futuristic year of 2000. Riordan smiled—now the distant past. Anyway, Bugs, his chips called in, begins to dig his own grave. But it's Elmer who witlessly gets buried of course and there in his grave he reflects that at least he's finally free of that cwazy wabbit. But then old-man Bugs pops his head through the soil and Riordan out-loud laughed.

"I told you."

"You did."

But it didn't last. He frowned.

Naive? Sentimental?

Which?

He breathed, thinking. Somehow vexed. He hit the PAUSE

button and struggled up out of her La-Z-Boy. Nuked another fortified chamomile in the kitchen and shoved open the fire door to the garage. The chill. Like the Lascaux caves.

There: on the kilned planks of his workbench, the chapbook. Where he'd left it those hundred and one nights before:

Death and the Butterfly: Nerudian Sonnets of Love and Deprivation by a Dead Airman as Whispered to Alexander Polo

On the chapbook's cover a jagged monolith of basalt jutting up from the swirls and froth of a sea; above the black rocks, a butterfly, but one evocative of a twin-engine plane—eerily evanescent—as it approaches in search of somewhere to light, to land. Isla Negra. His heart beginning to race, he turned to the table of contents. Ran his finger down, seeking something— doubtless somewhere to light, to land, during this: his own descent (though not yet demise):

Sonnet 3. Lost in the Forest
Sonnet 8. I Want to Look Back

No. The night of the reading. What had touched him? What? What?

Sonnet 11. Get Used to the Shadow

Not that either. But then:

Sonnet 13. I Do Not Love You

Was that it? He riffled through to the page. Was it? Was it?

I do not love you like deserts love the night

Yes. Yes. That was it.

or rivers love the fealty of their banks.

But it was the next two lines he sought, the lines that had haunted him, whispering like a mute ghost entombed in his soul:

I love you like violins love windows
that open onto orchards and pear blossoms.

An axe in his frozen sea, those lines. For had he? Loved her like violins love windows? Windows that open onto orchards? And pear blossoms? Had he? What about the—the day he left her at the altar? The stupid fucking motor coach. The stupid fucking trip. What about that, huh? Huh? Jesus. Violins? Fuck. Anything but. And he sobbed, sobbed and pinched the bridge of his nose with his fingertips. Sobbed again.

And then this:

Jack? Jack?

He looked up.

Bea?

Jack, my love. Do you know how many times you've apologized to me for that?

Too—too many?

Actually, nowhere nearly enough.

He laughed. Wiped his eyes of their drying tears.

You're just trying to cheer me up.

Me? Of course not. But if you want cheering up, then follow me.

To where?

Touch my hand.

Like this?

Yes. And bring the book.

Now, JONATHAN "JACK" RIORDAN—NOW ARE there voices. You can hear them in this cave, your bunker (aka your garage) as you follow her, voices building from inside your house: talk and chatter, polite and decorum'd but animated and exuberant enough. Even some laughter. And smitten and oh-so-willing you reopen the fire door and reenter the kitchen.

Lo! But it is daylight and a wake greets you. Hundreds of the mourning and the mournful throng through the kitchen and hallways and living room, mostly all dressed in the somber (if not sober) pastels of gray and faint black. As you move amongst them, none pay you heed; indeed you seem to passage through them as though through a mist, hovering, impervious:

Her memorial of course from back in early November, scant months before. A November Wednesday afternoon, one ablaze with sunshine and blood-colored leaves and now do you drift from the kitchen and into the hallway aiming for the living room and the eulogies: Metz's: "Missoula's Madame President"; John's: "My favorite of all my dad's addictions"; and of course Bob's—Captain Robert's: "Thanks to Jack here, no longer a single mom but for the rest of eternity *the* singular mother."

And now—now do you watch played out before you, like Bugs and Elmer, your own eulogy: Look: see yourself step forth, glass in hand (a Jameson and Perrier, half-and-half), sporting the pink Oxford cotton-cloth and lavender tie: your Big Sur wedding threads, sí? On this November day no lump lodges within your throat. Save the one in your heart. Watch as you clear your throat and see how the gathered throng— hundreds all—fall as mute and motionless as stone cats. There: graciously and without preamble you relate that during Bea's final days you had piteously crabbed to her that when it came to this death business, you weren't very good at being Irish. "She had kindly mocked me," you then confess to the throng.

"With due respect to the father here," you explain, referring to Father Kendall from Saint Michael's, "Bea told me in no uncertain terms that not only was I true Irish, but true Irish Catholic." And here—here do you lovingly enumerate Bea's terms with the fingers of your free hand. "You drink, she told me. You have sex without birth control. And you never ever go to Mass."

Amidst the laughter and applause, on that day you did raise your glass in silent and forever benediction.

See, Jack, she whispers in your ear. *Violins.*

Five

He was eating his lunch—carne mechada[16] washed down by a 2007 Don Melchor cabernet franc—at a café called El Cielo on Avenue Isidoro Dubournais, Isla Negra when the owner/chef visited to enquire about the quality of his meal. This was February a year later. Chile. February is our August in Chile and through the glass windows you could see the 4A parked at the curb, as blue as the Valparaiso skies but nowhere near as blue as that chef's blue eyes. She had dark hair that fell behind her shoulders to her mid-waist— "trellis locks," he thought. A simple sleeveless dress stitched from unbleached sackcloth that did so cling to the curves of her bodice and taut but lush backside that it might have been grafted onto her body as seamlessly as an apple its skin. Slingbacks, open-toed sandals. Most startling of all were her freckles, tiny fox-red blemishes which kissed the non-existent bridge

16. Pot roast stuffed with bacon and garlic and onion.

of her nose and like butterfly wings opened slightly outward beneath each of those blue eyes.

She spoke almost flawless English and she asked him if he had been to Neruda's museum (he had) and what he had liked best (their beautiful graves) and where he was from in America (she and her new husband had honeymooned in Cabo, she told him).

"A glass on the house, Señor Guapo?"

"Sí. Gracias."

To honor him thusly would require a fresh bottle of the cab franc and in two steps she was at the bar. The bottle stood on one of the upper shelves and she stretched up to reach it and her backside flexed like globes of firm cream and her heels lifted out of her sandals and a peach of succulence traveled for an eternity up each of her calves. He looked away, embarrassed at his voyeurism and even more so by the relish he had drawn from it.

And she? Did she feel his eyes? The sear and burn of them on her backside as she stretched up towards some shy and heedful heaven? Probably, but either way she turned and flashed a smile, waggling at him the bottle which she deftly uncorked.

"I'm Gabriella," she told him as she poured him a six-ounce glassful.

"And I—I'm Elmer," he managed, still embarrassed. "Elmer Fudd."

She laughed. A tiny droplet of the exquisite vintage escaped the bottle's lip and falling graced the white tablecloth like one of her freckles.

"Then enjoy your wabbit juice," she said.

She returned to her kitchen. He sat quietly moping as he mopped up the velvety sauce of his mechada with a toe from the basket of bread. Done, he polished off his Don Melchor and he brooded. The first step in any betrayal is the smallest yet most indelible—like ink on a bedsheet—and he settled the bill, and hours later on this the first top-down and blowsy night of his 6,500-mile journey home he gunned the 4A northward along Ruta 5, punishing the car until the Stromberg carbs shrieked and the supercharger thundered like gods at twilight and the speedometer needle grazed 127 and the high Andean winds tried and tried but failed to blow that stain from his sorrow.

III

MARGARET, LILY, LILY, ROSE

Marley was dead—an apparent suicide—and so His Majesty's private secretary now bore the burden to inform him. As too the others of the realm: the fallen. Those whose letters Sir Jeffrey, the private secretary, now held in his hand. Thusly did he stand in the tall doorframe of this room: the king's office no less, in Windsor Castle no less, and there at his desk in his fully dressed drabs was George VI himself, preoccupied, as would be any monarch whose lands were enduring such desperate siege. Above him, a chandelier glittered. Behind him a Rumford fireplace pulsed, a fire within, whose tall blood-orange flames sizzled and licked at the mantelpiece.

Sir Jeffrey waited a moment then brought his hand not holding the letters up to his mouth and coughed.

The king looked up.

"Suh—*Sir* Jeffrey," he managed.

"The letters, Majesty."

The king gestured, and Sir Jeffrey stepped forward, extending the letters, his Oxford-don features a mask of solemnity.

"Huh—*how* many?" the king asked before dismissing an answer with his own: "Of course, wuh—*one* would be too many."

He leaned back into the plush and spindled throne of his chair. His desk was a massive teak affair—as formidable as a small building—and on the broad roof of its top were cabinet papers and telegrams and, grouped about, several fountain pens and ink bottles. And, of course, two large and crystal ashtrays, quite filled. Beside it, the room's windows gave out onto the castle's inner quadrangle and garden, its lawns now covered with a thin skein of snow, a covering as delicate as a wedding veil. And with even less permanence.

In amongst all this, Sir Jeffrey somehow found a place on the desk for the letters and he set them there as though laying a babe in the bulrushes.

"Majesty."

The king stared at the letters. Letters of condolence. To the families of those fallen. Of the soldiers and sailors and aviators. Within these letters' freight of dirge and dread lay one in particular. It addressed as follows:

Mr and Mrs Charles William George McEwan

The text of this identical to each before and each forever after:

*The queen and I offer you our heartfelt sympathy in
your great sorrow. We pray that your country's grat-
itude for a life so nobly given in its service may bring
you some measure of consolation.*

Consolation? Consolation? How he longed for just one
letter—just one!—to so read:

*The queen and I offer you our heartfelt apolo-
gies for mistakenly declaring your son dead or
missing-and-presumed . . .*

But in this conflagration, none would Lazarus back from
oblivion—none of the 383,711 letters that he would read and
sign. (Yes, he silently read each and every one before signing it
George VI, R&I.[17] His duty. But then not.)

"And," Sir Jeffrey said, and did so quietly for he sensed the
source of his monarch's preoccupation, "the—the princess to
see you."

"Hmm?"

"The princess. Margaret Rose."

"Rose?"

"Yes, Majesty."

"She's here? Now?"

"Shall I show her in?"

"Only if shuh—*she's* forgotten the way."

17. Rex et Imperator (King and Emperor).

"And Mr. Churchill, Majesty?"

"Churchill? I—*tell* him he'll have to wait his turn."

"I meant, will he be having dinner with us tomorrow?"

"It—it was a joke."

"Of course, Majesty. And a fine one. But Mr. Churchill? Tomorrow?"

"Is it Thursday?"

"It's the Feast of Stephen, Majesty."

Here the king glanced at the pile of letters in wait. Consolation. He sighed.

"I'm hardly Weh—*Wen*ceslas," he said. He shut his eyes and touched his fingers into the desk blotter, the fingernails unbitten though severely clipped.

"And the princess, Majesty?"

"Sorry?"

"Margaret Rose, Majesty."

"Please."

Sir Jeffrey bowed his head slightly and with practiced grace turned and with a gloved hand fooph'd open the door. After a moment's pause, the young princess entered.

Princess Margaret—Rose to kith and kin—was and is the most forlorn of that most forlorn of families: forbidden in her twenties because of the blue-ness of her blood to marry the love of her life: the impeccably handsome Group Captain Peter Townsend, RAF. Forbidden first by her sister, Elizabeth, no less, then eventually by Parliament. Imagine. Ah, but that is years to come. For, look, here now she stands. The king's daughter. Margaret Rose. As alive as she will ever now be: ten years of age.

This day she wore, strangely, American blue jeans (the cuffs turned up once at the ankles, suggesting they were likely a gift, perhaps from none other than Mrs. Roosevelt herself) and above those jeans a collarless cotton blouse. Her thick hair raven'd back and set in a French braid. A comb of Tuscan beryl to secure said braid in place.

The king looked at her. Beckoned her forth. Margaret Rose hadn't quite yet overcome her shyness around her father when he was being Mr. King, so she hesitated in mid-step and mid-utterance.

She glanced behind her at Sir Jeffrey, searching his face.

"I—I haven't told him, Your Highness," Sir Jeffrey confessed to her.

"Tuh—*told* me what, Sir Jeffrey?"

"About Marley, Majesty."

"My Christmas present, Father."

"The goldfish?"

Famously frugal, this royal family had, during the war and especially during the siege of the blitz, become even more so. To the point that they saved their hand-soap slivers in glass beakers of water to coagulate into crude but reusable clumps. And to give a Daughter of the Realm a Christmas present of a mere goldfish.

"He jumped out of his bowl, Majesty."

"As—as would I," the king said. A moment passed. "*His* goldfish bowl," the king added. But in that moment, Sir Jeffery had quietly vanished.

The king looked at his daughter.

"Lillibet found him," she finally said.

"Marley?"

"Nana was reading to us from Dickens."

"Ah. Of course. Cuh—*come* here," he said. She hesitated. "Come on."

Stiff-legged as a foal, she navigated around the desk, her crisp jeans rustling like sails. He held his hands out, palms up, and reaching him she placed hers—small and pink as petals—in his larger: gray and lined. His life. The hands tender nonetheless, no matter their call or service.

"Lillibet—"

"What, my precious?"

"Well, we—we got into a bit of a row?"

"Really? You two?"

"Yes, father."

"And what was this bit of a row about, then? Hmm?"

"About ghosts, Papa."

"And what about them?"

"Well, Nana was reading us—"

"Yes, from Dickens. And?"

"His *Christmas Carol*. And when Nana told us there were ghosts even here, here in the castle, well, Lillibet scolded Nana that there are no ghosts. Not here. Not anywhere. None at all in real life. Only in silly stories."

"She—she may be Lillibet most of the time, but she's also Elizabeth, after all."

"Yes, Papa, but—"

"But what?" the king asked.

"But I—I want there to be ghosts."

"Sorry?"

"Yes. I *want* there to be ghosts."

Now the king hadn't the foggiest of what to say next. His little Rose petal *wanted* there to be ghosts? So in wan compensation he resorted as we all do—to our somnambulant addictions—and he drew out from his breast pocket his silver cigarette case and snapped open the clasp and slinked out a cigarette. He clipped shut the case and set it on his desk beside the condolence letters and lit the cigarette. He inhaled. Chronic smokers inhabit the same maddening liturgy as chronic drinkers, and the king exhaled as exactly as he had that day at the window with Churchill, his lips exuding a gorgeous peninsula of gray.

You mean London? The City? The people themselves?

At the same instant he glanced at the letters. Of condolence. Those signed and those yet in wait.

The people themselves?

Good Christ! Ghosts? How many had he, stuttering little twerp Bertie Windsor, accumulated? Or forged, like the links in the chains that Marley's ghost had raised and rattled at the terrified Scrooge?

Such moments take a lifetime, and our lifetimes are spare, save such moments, and the king inhaled again, his eyes and mind alight upon the letters, the one buried within that concerns us here:

Mr and Mrs Charles William George McEwan
Kenton, Middlesex

Ghosts. The king averted his head to the side and exhaled, this one a narrow and shimmering slipstream that rolled and tumbled, like un-nesting Russian dolls, through the chandelier'd air.

"*I'll* smoke someday," the Princess pronounced.

This startled the king, like a shade in a door knocker and brought him, at least temporarily, back to earth. And he appraised now his younger daughter: ten going on one-and-twenty.

"Buh—*but* why would you want there to be ghosts? Especially here—here in the castle."

"So I can capture one."

"You can't capture ghosts. Even if there were such creatures."

"Oh, but I can. I mean, I could. I'm Margaret—Margaret Rose. Of the Royal House of Windsor."

"Indeed you are, my precious. But why—why would you want to capture one? A ghost?"

"So I could make it teach me."

"Teach you what?"

She was quiet. Uncertain.

"Well?" he asked.

She frowned, summoning her resolve.

"How—how to fly," she declared.

The king laughed at this—no, he is Bertie, beloved father—thus did he laugh not at it but *with* it.

"But you already know," he told his younger daughter.

"I do?"

"Yes," he said, and he spread his king'd and soldiered arms wide—wide as the wings of Gabriel.

"Come," he said, beckoning, "come see for yourself."

L et us now leave this furrowed king and his princess to their embrace and like Icarus and Daedalus take flight though not over the kingdom of Minos and the Aegean, but over time: eleven years and the meadows of Runnymede, grasses that run a league west along the Thames from Windsor Castle. There in those meadows now stands the tomb of the lost airmen, Runnymede's Air Forces Memorial; a tomb for those 20,288 who rest in no known burial place.

And this day? This is the seventeenth of October 1953—the day of the memorial's dedication. A shroud of cloud paints out sky and sun, denying the ground of its shadows. A damp chill pervades, a chill and dampness that women in particular feel, especially in the marrow of their ankles and especially if they are wearing high heels and nylon stockings, as are almost all this day. Mothers and wives. Daughters. Those of the fallen airmen.

But ah, the edifice itself: built of white stone whose great doors reveal a hushed courtyard of trimmed grass and living wreaths of color. In the courtyard's center, the Stone of Remembrance. The towerlike shrine itself. All this cloistered in the eternal embrace of the 342 panels whereon are writ the names of the dead. The panels: two-story-tall stone pages facing each other, like those of a great book engraved on a Mount and left intentionally open. For all time. To be so read and revered. By those gathered.

Amongst those gathered today are sisters. Two in particular. One, in black belted coat and matching cloche hat, the sister of Princess Rose, now grown and now none other than Elizabeth Regina: queen of all England. A simple string of pearls around her neck. As she moves through the throng, offering words of grace and condolence to many, she stops in front of another sister: Susan, younger sister of Flight Lieutenant Phillip McEwan and now titled Mrs. Roger Grey. Clad for the inclemency in a belted coat of dark burgundy, unadorned save for the Royal Air Corps lapel pin of her father's. Her head too unadorned save for its startling tangle of tendril'd dark hair. The rich red lips. The moist eyes. But beside this sister of woe, the true bearer of pall: the mother, Cless, in her Sunday-best Mackintosh, lipstick, makeup, and silk kerchief adorned with a print of white carnations. Widowed twice within months. Her face lined by the streets of loss and sorrow.

Silence.

The queen looks at these two women, crippled on this occasion by their grief, a grief spawned more than a decade distant, and for an instant she is no longer Elizabeth Regina, but

Lillibet, and she sees now in their eyes the flight and mystery of it all, and for a moment she loses if not her poise then at least her certainty. No ghosts? Not even here in this legend place? Where here in this same meadow her long-ago ancestor John, as querulous as a colic, nonetheless signed the Magna Carta Libertatum? Or here where her late father, Bertie, George the VI, brought her and her sister Rose to pay homage to that great signing mere days after the unconditional surrender of Nazi Germany? Can she not see them? Her father dressed in matching tweed coat and breeks (breeches); she and her sister in wool cardis and plaid skirts; the three of them marching across the grass and the May blue skies in bright-red Wellies, father and daughters in perfect step and swinging their arms like Christopher Robins on parade and all three wearing faces filled not with the jubilation of victory but with the astonishment of their survival and the weightlessness of their relief.

Ghosts? And not just those of past and present, but what about the future? Susan's that is. The future ghosts of her betrayal—hovering above that bed in Trail like bottled madness? Above the nose-cone wreckage of that most fleeting of graves? Or the ghosts of her diagnosis: in the doctor's office as she and Roger sit like Tussaud figurines: *Lewy body disease. And—and the cure? To sleep? Perchance to dream?* Or those above the motor coach when indeed they do their quietus make. The motor coach parked within the lush banks of the shimmering Clark Fork. They hold glasses and listen to Bach's Concerto for Two Violins, the Largo ma non tanto, of course. Their glasses? Twin teacups. China: Spode, Blue Willow. The cocktail within? Quinalbarbitone (Seconal): fifteen grams dissolved in an elixir of Calvados and cyclobenzaprine (a muscle relaxant). But give listen: The Academy of Ancient Music recording: the tone and timbre of the ancient violins and accompanying strings so wrenching and aching that even the dead can hear and doing so do copiously weep. *Our Mr. Polo? No, my love. We've missed him? Slings and arrows.*

Indeed, ghosts—and worlds—to come. Far, far too soon enough.

But return us now to the living: to the queen. No longer Lillibet but Elizabeth again she asks the elder of her two subjects, "Your son?"

The mother shuts her eyes and nods then glances at the young woman at her side. "And her brother," she tells her monarch.

The young queen now lowers her own eyes and, in a voice as quiet and breaking as all three ravaged hearts, says to them, "My—my sympathy."

And then she moves on.

IN MEMORIAM EST

Susan Lindsay Urquat Grey (née McEwan)
RN
b: 29 August 1927
d: 15 August 2000

Beatrice (Bea) Ireland Tully Sims
BMgmt, CPA, MBA, Professor Emeritus,
U. Montana
b: 08 August 1939
d: 15 October 2012

Shoshanna (Shoshe) Lara Polo
Child
b: 14 February 1984
d: 29 November 1984

ADDENDUM

THE POEMS

Suzanne, the Name

Suzanne, the name: with it, Tintoretto
and Rembrandt swirled the lipsticks of their palettes
into the gradual white of lilies:
a white with the longing of mirrors.

Even the Bible aches for its return,
to hold again, in its passages, that name,
its sentence of death for adultery,
the trees from which hung its accusers.

O name: alighting from the night skies
on convoys of silence, it sailed
long as a ship forged solely from vowels,

sailed right through me, divining my compass,
the manners of my evening, spoke
in iambs its secret, daring me follow.

I Did Not Hold Your Night

I did not hold your night, the trees that spoke
announcing in the green flares of their leaves:
your birth, the books you slept in, the saltless sea
upon which you ran, shunning its black sand.

No. Imposter of love that I am,
I found your eyes in Cinque Terre,
your sandals from Toscana,
the voice, in your hips when you dance, from Cadiz.

Ages I wore this mask—ages—afraid
of you. Afraid of the long procession
of fields you have so summarily dismissed.

Poets have sung of love's understanding,
but I, feebly, mention only your ankles:
golden as scythes, slashing in Bolívar's sun.

Lost in the Forest

Lost in the forest, I broke off a branch
of sunlight, and heard in its spilling blood:
your fears. Or those of your distant sisters,
the swans, thrushing like doves through the trees above.

That light, prophetic as a comet, moved
seeking the coal in me, smiling at my grave,
a smile saddened by the fate of evergreens:
by their darkness and outstretched, orphan arms.

They neither sleep, nor dream, nor die, proclaimed
that minted yellow light, *they are perfume
that climbs and climbs and climbs but never flies.*

Like dead lovers buried side by side, they
embrace only themselves, never the other—
unlike you, cringing on the edge of skies.

Come with Me

Come with me, I said and waited—waited
until the moon, like a stone that is warm
in frozen water, slowly descended
and touched the earth with the terror of horses.

I said it again, whispering: Come with me?
and around me arose from the reefs
of the seas a thousand shipwrecks, oozing
cannons of emeralds and water and blood.

So, when I heard you say, Come with me?
The moon returned to its shelf in the heavens,
the wrecked ships dissolved 'neath the reefs of the seas,

and my heart galloped, faster and faster
until I could taste in my mouth: your words,
and copper and death—all sweet as leather.

If Your Eyes

If your eyes were stolen by the moon
so that it might look upon you and *not* weep;
if your step—your carriage—were instead the trees';
if you had never owned your trellis locks,

or the soft lions that awake in your waist
when you dream and forget you must breathe;
if you were not a tall, sleek basket
of danger woven from strawberry, from clove,

how, my precious, could I not still love you?
Not love the slow hands that would now be your eyes?
The wind-vane sway of your motionless feet?

The sound of the sky in your untressed nape?
Not your waist? Breathless, sleepless, and lean?
Or your scent—unrivaled—like wine in a cave!

Naked, You Are

Naked, you are a swimming, distant world,
a bare island on the horizon
of a green star: afloat, with no shadow.
Naked you are as supple as kilned sand.

Naked, you are as cautious as a dream
of mollusks and ravens, or unborn fires.
Naked, you are the blades of sunset
and sunrise, high noon, midnight, and moonrise.

Naked you can crook one knee, and your body
becomes contained within the smooth chancel
of your leg, a pause in a sermon of want.

In that pause, wandering like someone
marooned in a map, I stagger without breath,
naked, under that hungering green star.

Suzanne, Where Are You?

Suzanne, where are you? I mean, years from now
as you read this? For yes, we dead are flightless,
without shiver or heat, yet our hearts—
empty as footprints—still crave what has been.

Do you stand on the sly carpet of gill
in your greenhouse, its panes caulked with menace?
Or do you stroll your high gardens, this page,
torn like a butterfly, on your sleeve?

Or perhaps there is snow, the flakes knitted
like wool on the stalking tails of your
leopards. How I hunger, Suzanne: where are you?

Massifs of time stand between us—like pharaohs.
But through their blue heights I *now* see you falling
in love—in love with that distance between us.

I Want to Look Back

I want to look back and see you on the cross;
or, sitting on your heels beneath it,
gaming with the momentary soldiers,
your silk cloak hung on an ankle nail.

The men will not raw your bare shoulders
with their knuckled grunts, for you are luminous
to them: your hair brighter than the lightning
that tills the dark and far-off waste of hills.

But one, with the smile of a lion, will fill
his helmet with cold black wine and, rising
in his clanging robe of armor, feel

the heat of your beauty—your face: a rose
on fire—and offer his helmet's annealed freight
to the punctured figure, towering above.

The Light That Rises

The light that rises when you awaken
wakens too and finds, each time, it needs
to know you—know you as it must a flower
growing on the surface of the sun.

What would this flower be? Tall daffodil?
Slender nard? Or a flower not yet known:
a flower of mist, ivory, soft pearl,
a flower that can blush, that can—die?

Your death—the words are lightless on my tongue.
Yet, would I mourn? For though I would not have
this flower forever, nor would no other.

No, die you must not. There on the surface
of the sun—amidst a thousand seas of flame—
the light wakens, and death and tears and I burn.

You Will Remember

You will remember the Flood, when the rain
poured from the rocks in a sea, and a lone
gondolier saw in the throat of a dove:
cities in the vast plains, pillared in salt.

You will remember the burial in Qin
of six thousand armed statues, a parade
of stone soldiers interred in the hills
like the relentless roots of the tree of war.

You will even remember the earth
whorled into being, by Shiva and Yahweh,
from that first wet dust, thick as moss on the stars.

But you will not remember our stillness,
our blindness, our print in the grass of desire.
Never, never will you remember.

Get Used to the Shadow

Get used to the shadow of my shadow;
accept that the ageless snow falling
falls desiring to sustain the imprint
of our two bodies on your silent sheets.

For desire requires neither blood nor poems
nor the precipitous assemblage
of owls, moons, and stars. Desire requires
only time, distance, and the coals of the heart.

For you, my desired, never arrive.
You do not emerge from the doors of the earth,
nor descend through the portals of nigh.

Even in death I will loiter, waiting,
listening for the softly falling fruit
of your footsteps, the long knife of your eyes.

Perhaps Nothingness Is

Perhaps nothingness is your heartbeat
no longer within my reach, my ear:
like a poem emptied suddenly
and utterly of its sounds, its silence.

Perhaps nothingness is *my* heartbeat
no longer within *your* reach, *your* hearing:
solitary as the drip drip of rain
on the tile and terrace of a ruin.

What else can I hear when I listen?—
but the mouthfuls of apricot sun
you once whispered—now seashells without shores.

Perhaps our hearts while they beat are nothing
but a struggle to be still—your heart
still struggling as I listen, listen.

I Do Not Love You

I do not love you like deserts love the night
or rivers love the fealty of their banks.
I love you like violins love windows
that open onto orchards and pear blossoms.

I love you how the knees of the earth
sink with certitude into their beddings
of mole tunnels, rose thorns, butterfly wings,
feeling the soft yield and crisp bite of marsh nights.

I love you with the blood of my future;
I love you with the slow flame of my past;
I love you because I cannot remember

how not to: how to creep past your silence,
the steeples and fingers of your hands
calling out, beckoning, pleading for deafness.

You Sing

You sing even when you are dreaming,
when you are bathing, when you cry;
when you tease bread, beguile wine; when you lie
like deep snow lies in the eaves of your castles.

The world could be calmed like a field of gray monks,
robed in their motionless salutes and their
gathering eyes—calm as the demise of death,
the green winter that waits without eulogy.

Yet *still* would you sing—sing like the archer
who hunts not with his bow or his arrow
but with the sound of his unstrung bowstring.

Yes, your voice—it wavers in my memory
like a leaf in the deepest forest
of the ocean, farther, farther from shore.

Of All the Stars

Of all the stars I admired, flanged
across the quick flints of winter's sky,
I sought the warmth of but one, and my life,
lit by time and savage heart, glowed.

Of all the waves that seamed through me,
I swam in the undertow of your moisture,
not drowning, not breathing, but drinking
the unbrined purity of your goodbyes.

The sea and the sky are lovers—lovers!
Ones who have never danced, never met:
lovers who have never hidden from themselves

their unbreakable solace. We though, now,
afeared of fire, athirst for sorrow, meet and
dance only in the slow parlors of demise.

I Hunt for a Sign of You

I hunt for a sign of you: in the vast shelves
of the unborn—the blind and starling girls:
those knot-kneed stalks of women who will grope
the drained and darkened hallways of ungiven love.

There! I see one: she pendulums down
in vessel braid from cane, from eyelash
and from mirth; tiny as a fledgling star,
nascent and pure and fragile as pond ice.

You (who know more about banishment
than all the sired of Earth's dispatched
and descried), you must dray and gather her;

cradle her; translate the secret meter
of verse she will write long before she bathes
herself in the marsh of ache and confusion.

When I Die

When I die, I want your hands to weep,
your breasts to avert their eyes, the huntress
in your heart to kneel and grasp in grace her prey—
yes: the full monument of your darkest clay.

And I want you to live—live in the same caves
and rains where the ash of our two names
first caught fire; where the words of our love
first caught—in your throat, like a moth in moonlight.

Believe me this: you will blossom and flower
as never before. Your face with its thousand
exquisite petals in every shade

of rose and of pink, so pure that your eyes,
blazed with azure, will see, with each love
you transcend, my bones in the distance.

Age Covers Us

Age covers us the way prayer covers graves,
the way sleep grafts the opaque skin of dreams,
the way fallen leaves, tasted by rains,
foretell, like footprints, each of our betrayals.

Lovers, like all who are lost, look back
as surely you must. Look!: your fingers trembling
on the belted loops of your waist, on
the lips of our hunger, our grieving.

This is the way flesh consumes itself,
the way time bleeds itself, the way our eyes
cast themselves off the cliffs of our longing.

For the hours do not distinguish between
the pear and the blossom, between the dance
and the slipper—the forlorn, the forgotten.

In the Center of the Earth

In the center of the earth, I would stand
in the rain that pours through the umbrella
of graves far above: stand until you came—
came walking with your face raised like cupped hands.

The rain, every drop written by the dead,
will darken the ropes of the greenery,
launch caskets of swimming petals and leaves,
and cling in a wedding gown to your skin.

For a moment, only you will exist,
the rain about you like crystal wings,
coating you with a glaze of diamonds.

And there, as you lower your gaze and see
me, you'll taste—as alights from above
the butterfly of death—my lives on your tongue.

COLIN HESTER is a British-born former student of Zen and former thirty-year-old paperboy. The author of *Diamond Sutra*, Hester has taught writing at Central Washington University, the University of Montana, and the University of Colorado. He lives just north of Seattle with his British-born wife and his U.S.-born cat. Find out more at colinhester.com